Praise for
SOINBHE LAL[...]
A Hive for the H[...]

★ "Based on the real world of the honeybee, this unusual fantasy is humorous and profound. Reminiscent of Richard Adams's *Watership Down* in its artful and complete creation of the world of an animal group, Lally's novel also holds a mirror to our society. Who is in charge here? Why do we continue to act as if other creatures are our enemies? What is the reason for our life? What is our destiny? Why do we die? . . . Memorable in every way."

—*School Library Journal*, starred review

"A tight compelling read."

—*The New York Times Book Review*

"Lally lyrically describes the natural setting, as well as fascinating details about the care and upkeep of a hive. Her gently humorous and touching portraits of Belle, Thora, and the rest will endear these characters to young readers, while the escalating drama, leading up to a war with the wasps, will keep pages turning. And the icing on the cake: this is a beautifully designed volume, with pencil-drawn chapter heads by Brewster that are both amusing and delicate."

—*Publishers Weekly*

■ "*Antz* meets *Animal Farm* in this allegory about the work women and men do to keep civilization humming. . . . Young people who pick this up will find an inventive and thoughtful novel. Along with the interesting character interaction, Lally is also meticulous in her re-creation of hive life."

—*Booklist*, boxed review

"Comparisons to *Animal Farm* are a given here, although Lally's bee-hive is a more universal allegory for our common social and political ills. . . .Lally does not shirk from the gorier details of hive business. . . . Illustrations of spindly-legged bees with human features further reveal individual personalities, and lively dialogue brings the hive to life."

—*The Horn Book*

Other Signature Titles

Ghost Cats
Susan Shreve

Bad Girls
Cynthia Voigt

Bat 6
Virginia Euwer Wolff

P.S. Longer Letter Later
Ann M. Martin and Paula Danziger

The Music of Dolphins
Karen Hesse

Out of the Dust
Karen Hesse

A Hive for the Honeybee

Soinbhe Lally

Illustrations by
Patience Brewster

SCHOLASTIC
Signature

an imprint of
Scholastic Inc.

New York Toronto London Auckland Sydney
Mexico City New Delhi Hong Kong

ISBN 0-590-51045-2

Text copyright © 1996 by Soinbhe Lally.
Illustrations copyright © 1999 by Patience
Brewster. All rights reserved. Published by
Scholastic Inc. by arrangement with Poolbeg Press
Ltd. SCHOLASTIC and associated logos are
trademarks and/or registered trademarks of
Scholastic Inc.

12 11 10 9 8 7 6 5 4 3 2   1 2 3 4 5 6/0

Printed in the U.S.A.   40

First Scholastic paperback printing, May 2001

Original hardcover edition designed by
Marijka Kostiw, published by
Arthur A. Levine Books, an imprint of
Scholastic Press, February 1999

MANY THANKS TO BEEKEEPERS PETER
O'REILLY AND MY SISTER ANNA, WHO
SHARED WITH ME THEIR KNOWLEDGE
AND EXPERIENCE.

TO THE MEMORY OF MY FATHER, WHO ALWAYS TOLD HIS BEES WHEN THERE WAS AN IMPORTANT EVENT IN THE FAMILY. IF THE BEES WERE NOT TOLD ABOUT BIRTHS, MARRIAGES, AND DEATHS THEY MIGHT, ACCORDING TO TRADITIONAL BEE LORE, LEAVE THE HIVE — OR DIE.

Nine bean-rows will I have there, a hive

   for the honeybee,

And live alone in the bee-loud glade.

W. B. YEATS
"The Lake Isle of Innisfree"

for two days the hive had sung the
song of the swarm. The brood combs were filled
with young and the honeycombs were brim-
ming with honey. In the orchard outside, nettles
ran to flower in the neglected grass. Brambles

grew riotously in the corners, their pale blossoms heavy with the weight of nectar and black pollen.

The bees were restless. They idled at the entrance of the hive, ignoring the few field bees who still came and went with the harvest. They bustled about without actually doing anything and fed freely on the carefully hoarded stores of honey. When a perfect day dawned, and the early sun shone warm on the threshold of the hive, excitement rose to fever pitch. It was time to leave.

However, the old Queen refused to go. Worker bees crowded around her, urging her toward the entrance, but still she resisted. "The young ones," she pleaded, "we cannot leave them untended."

"They are provided for," an attendant reassured her. "Now you must come away. The hive is overcrowded. We will start again, somewhere new."

"No," the Queen exclaimed violently, "I don't want to go." She pushed her way through the cortege of attendant bees and made her way back to the brood. At the edge of the comb, she paused. The scent of honey hung heavily in the amber darkness. "I must stay here," she insisted, "it's where I belong."

Her attendants crowded around her once more. They stroked her wings and caressed her antennae. The senile old Queen became placid and forgot the anguish of a moment before. She hummed contentedly. Gently her attendants led her forward.

Thinking she was being brought to a new brood comb, she submitted. However, when she realized that she was being led toward the white light of the outside world, she struggled again to turn back. Her escort surrounded her with a living cage of wings and nudged her out through the entrance, onto the threshold of the hive. A steady stream of bees flowed outward and gathered around her. Thousands rose in the air, their singing loud and joyful.

It was almost noon. The air was warm and filled with scents of summer. For almost an hour the swarm hovered in a dense, humming cloud above the hive till the Queen, wearied by unaccustomed flight, flew to rest on the bole of an ancient apple tree. The swarm followed and surrounded her, a black humming mass, suspended between the bole of the tree and one of its leafy boughs.

Scouts went away from the swarm to seek a site for a new hive. They came back with reports of a hollow in a tree, a cranny in a limestone wall, an enclosed space under a loose roof tile. The swarm sang in dizzy excitement. A decision was made. Then the black cloud detached itself from the apple tree and flew away from the old orchard with its lichen-hung trees. Humming loudly, it crossed a meadow, passed through a gap in a whitethorn hedge and along a reedy riverbank, till at last its sound faded and it disappeared from sight.

2

back in the hive, Thora stood
on the edge of the stores of ripening honey and
fanned her wings incessantly. She had fanned all
day in spite of the commotion and excitement.
The song of the swarm had hummed all around
her but she remained dutifully at her post. She

was a house bee, just three days old. When she listened to the song of the swarm, she longed to follow the old Queen into the world outside, but she knew she could not. She was one of the chosen ones who would remain in the hive, keepers of its future, of the new brood and the wealth of honey that it would provide for them.

Only the day before she had assumed fanning duties. Since then she had paused once to sleep briefly, and only once again to make a cleansing flight out of the hive.

She felt enormously conscious of the importance of fanning, although she longed to rest her aching wings for just an instant. If she were to neglect her task the wax combs would overheat and melt. The honey and brood that they contained would be destroyed. Returning field bees would lose their way.

It was only three days, but already it seemed a long time since she had torn open the capping of the wax cell where she was born. She could vaguely remember that she had once been a small, ravenous larva, tended by nurse bees who fed her bee milk and later honey and pollen. She

grew big, almost filling her wax cell. Then
she spun her cocoon, and house bees capped her
cell with pollen and wax. For twelve days she
slept.

When she tore the capping from her cell and
emerged into the hive, she found she had grown
six legs and two pale, dusty wings. Gingerly she
crawled onto the brood comb. There was darkness all around, but she could feel and smell
other bees working busily on all sides. She could
hear them and with her small middle eye she
could discern their shapes and movements. She
was hungry after her long fast and held out her
tongue to passing workers, but they ignored her.
Again and again she held out her tongue to one
and then another.

"Do keep out of the way," an irate house bee
said.

"But I'm hungry."

"Oh, very well." The house bee regurgitated
honey and offered it on her tongue.

"Thanks," Thora said, sipping gratefully.
The honey made her feel stronger. She suddenly
realized that she was dusty, and cleaned and

groomed herself, carefully brushing her body hair and cleaning her wings.

She spent the first two days of her life cleaning brood cells. Toward the end of the second day the weather grew warm and some fanning bees asked her to help them fan. She had been fanning ever since.

All around her was the heavy scent of ripe willow honey, which had been harvested months ago, during the first sunny days of spring. While she fanned, her head hummed with the music of the hive. The bees had resumed their accustomed song after the departure of the swarm, and went about their usual chores.

Late in the afternoon, Belle came. Belle was two days older than Thora. As a mark of her maturity, she had just been appointed a hive cleaner. It was her job to sweep up the dust made by a hundred thousand busy feet coming and going on the hive floor all day. She helped keep the combs tidy and carried old broken honeycomb out of the hive. She enjoyed the authority her new position gave her, and made a great deal of noise as she attended to her duties.

"Filthy drones," she scolded, crossing a comb and surveying the mess the male bees had made when they plundered the honey that morning. She turned to Thora, who was the bee nearest to her. "They never take a cleansing flight, you know. Just leave their droppings anywhere. Filthy things."

"But isn't that the way drones are?" Thora suggested timidly. "They need us workers to take care of them."

"They're lazy and useless," Belle said indignantly. "Just look at this." She showed Thora a turd coated with honey. A drone had defecated right inside a honey cell.

"Disgusting."

Not all of the drones had left with the swarm. Some had grown too drunk on honey and had fallen asleep on the rim of the combs. "Come on, move yourself," Belle said, prodding a sleeping drone who was almost twice as big as herself. "Get off, I have to clean up here. Go on, scoot."

The drone looked at her, bleary-eyed. "My Queen," he murmured blissfully, "my Queen."

"I'm not your Queen," Belle said, giving him another indignant poke. "Come on, get out of here."

He crawled docilely across the top of the comb, paused at an open honey cell, and plunged his head deep into it.

"Get off. I have to clean up this mess you've made," Belle said angrily, and pushed him away from the honey.

He withdrew his head from the honey cell. "Just a moment," he said good humoredly and plunged his head in once more. "There," he said at last with a belch of satisfaction. "Be a good girl, wipe me down."

"Can't you wipe yourself down?" Belle was exasperated.

In reply he shook his body from side to side and stamped his legs in a grooming invitation dance. "Please, please, clean me," he chanted rhythmically. It was impossible to resist a grooming invitation dance. In spite of herself, Belle found herself brushing down his horny hair and wiping his antennae. He sighed with pleasure and spread out his wings to let her clean out the awkward place between the thorax and the abdomen. Belle scolded indignantly as she cleaned the last of the honey off his abdomen and finally pushed him away from the honey-comb. "Now stay out of here for a while and let me get this place cleaned up."

Thora watched with interest. She had seen drones occasionally coming and going to be fed and groomed and she slept close to them when the bees clustered together in the brood chamber at night. However she had never spoken to a male bee, till the confusion of today's swarming brought them roistering up through the brood combs and into the honey stores.

This drone seemed to be an idiot, a nice idiot. When he came that morning for honey he had taken the trouble to introduce himself with a polite little bow to each of the fanning bees on the edge of the comb.

"Won't you join me?" he asked each in turn. The workers refused.

"My name's Alfred," he said to Thora. "Are you sure you'll not uncap a honey cell with me? Join me in a little tipple?"

Thora shook her head. "I really can't. I have to fan. But do have a nice honey binge. There's lots of honey in the stores behind the brood."

Alfred blundered off, leaving Thora bemused. She couldn't help liking him. He was such a big, handsome, charming fellow. Even if drones did plunder the honey and leave it messed up and uncapped, that was just their way. Workers didn't really mind tidying up after them. Drones were so helpless and incompetent. Someone had to look after them.

Belle cleaned furiously. She felt angry, desperately angry.

"Don't let those stupid drones get you down," a friend said.

"They don't mean any harm," Thora added, careful not to interrupt her fanning while joining in the conversation.

"It's not the drones, that's not it at all," Belle replied.

"Then what is it?"

"The Queen. We have no Queen." She stopped working and raised her voice in a sorrowful wail.

Thora was so dismayed that she stopped fanning. The cleaners stopped cleaning. Belle's song released a flood of grief in each of them, and they raised their voices in unison. The drones who had fallen asleep in the passageway were roused by the unaccustomed noise. One by one, they woke from their honey-drunkenness and joined in, singing a deeper, more despairing song. The workers sang a lament for the loss of the mother of the hive. The drones sang their own heartbreaking song, a song of lost love.

Night fell. The sound of grief spread through the combs, and soon there echoed on all sides the sorrowful song of a hive bereft of its Queen.

the following afternoon the drones
congregated about the threshold of the hive.
The fine weather continued and the air was
warm. A good many drones just wanted to hover
in the sunshine but others, more energetic, felt
that an emergency meeting should be held.

"Are we all here?" somebody asked.

They looked around. A lot of drones were missing. They were the ones who had been sober enough to go away with the swarm. They carefully checked their numbers to see who had actually stayed behind.

"We will need a chairdrone," an elder drone said. He immediately appointed himself chairdrone to keep the meeting in order, and alighted on a prominent spot on the roof of the hive. "It is essential," he announced gravely, "to secure the government of the hive."

Some elder drones hovered close around him and there was a brief consultation. After a few minutes the chairdrone announced that he and several other elder drones would form a Grand Council, which would govern the hive. He himself would assume the position of Grand Drone.

A few younger drones demurred. Their leader was Mo, a two-week-old drone who had already shown a talent for discussion and disputation in the course of the daily convocations of drones around the threshold of the hive. "Wouldn't it be more democratic to vote?" he objected.

The newly-appointed Grand Drone of the Grand Council of Drones scowled in his direction.

"I mean," Mo persisted, "if drones are equal and all that, shouldn't we all have a say?"

"Certainly all drones are equal," a Council member conceded, "but it is customary for young drones to defer to wisdom and experience."

"Unfortunately some young drones are notably lacking in both," the Grand Drone added in a severe tone.

There was a loud hum of agreement from the assembly. Most of the drones there were more than two weeks old.

Mo, crushed, withdrew from the argument. During the half hour that followed, appointments were made and insignificant drones were elevated to important positions.

Mo, however, was passed over.

His friend Alfred fared better. Alfred was a fat bumbling drone with an eccentric way of using words and phrases. "It's poetry," he would explain when other drones asked what on earth he meant. Now the Grand Council made his eccentricity official by appointing him Laureate of the Hive. They immediately commissioned him to write a poem. As Laureate, it would be his first official duty to express, in poetry, the grief of the hive at the loss of their Queen.

Mo tried not to mind. "I wouldn't want to work for the Grand Council," he told himself, "they can keep their stupid jobs."

The assembly then debated the emergency situation. A senior drone flew up and alighted near the Grand Drone. He waited till the Grand Drone nodded, giving him permission to speak.

"Gentledrones," he said in the silky voice of an experienced orator, "we are here to express our grief at the loss of our Queen, mother of the hive and of each one of us assembled here." He paused and bowed his head. Each drone did the same. Then he sighed deeply and continued, "However, we must not despair. We must now look to the future of the hive. What we need is a young Queen, a young virgin Queen."

The proposal was received with enthusiastic applause.

"But how will we get a virgin Queen," Mo asked loudly as the applause faded, "which of you can tell us that?"

There was an uneasy silence. Drones looked from one to another to see if anyone knew.

"We'll go Queen-questing," someone said.

"And then?"

At first nobody replied. Then several drones tried to speak at once. "Order," the Grand Drone called above the din.

"Would the workers know anything about it?" a very young drone asked, and was shouted down by indignant elders.

"Order, order," the Grand Drone exclaimed over and over. No one paid any attention to him, and as the sun slanted across the orchard, lengthening the shadows of the apple trees, the meeting broke up and the drones scattered in disorderly groups.

for two days Alfred struggled to compose a poem. Deep within his being he knew that he thought more sublime thoughts than any other drone, he felt more sublime feelings, he dreamed more sublime dreams. When he spoke his sublime insights they became poetry. It just came naturally to him. Now he would have to tell of his sublime love for the departed Queen and his pain at losing her. And although his poem would be deeply personal, it would also be universal, since all drones shared his loss.

He worked for a long while. As his poem took shape he was overcome more than once by emotion. Whenever that happened he had to stop composing and console himself with honey. On the first day he was overcome with emotion so often that he became drunk and spent the afternoon sleeping. On the second day he drank less and composed more. As a result he did not complete his poem until the third day.

He repeated the poem again and again until he was satisfied that it expressed perfectly what he meant to say. Sometimes, as he repeated it, he was overcome yet again with emotion. This, however, was a different emotion caused, not by the loss of his Queen, but by the knowledge that he had composed a poem that was close to sublime.

"I've finished my poem," he announced to Mo.

"Which poem is that?" Mo asked. He knew perfectly well but disdained, on principle, to concern himself with the affairs of the Grand Council.

"My poem about our departed Queen."

"Oh that poem."

"Don't you want to hear it?"

"Please yourself."

With deep emotion Alfred spoke it aloud:

> The willow blossom
> Which gave
> The pale first nectar of spring
> Has withered now
> And its seed
> Floats on the summer breeze.

There was a pause. He waited for Mo to comment. "Well?" he asked when Mo said nothing.

"That's it?"

"Yes, that's it." Alfred was irritated. What

was wrong with Mo? Couldn't he feel all that emotion? Had he not listened properly?

"But it's not about the Queen, is it?" Mo pointed out. "It's about a willow."

"Of course it's about the Queen. The willow is a metaphor. It signifies the Queen."

"A metaphor?"

"Yes, she's like the willow blossom that brings us the first honey of spring."

"But she never brought us honey. The workers did that."

"That's not the point." Why did Mo have to be so literal?

"Then what is the point?"

Alfred tried to explain. "The Queen was as important to us as the first honey from the willow."

"Why didn't you just say so?"

"Because if I just said so it wouldn't be a poem, would it?"

He went to recite his poem to the Grand Council which was in session, hanging in midair above the center of the threshold board. Members of the Council had just accorded themselves the privilege of hovering above the best part of the threshold, right in the flight path of incoming field bees, where they could ask to sample the latest nectar harvest. When Alfred approached them they were noisily discussing affairs of state and kept him waiting. Eventually they found time to hear his poem.

"Go ahead," the Grand Drone said graciously.

Alfred recited his poem in an even voice, yielding only once to the emotion that had inspired it. When he finished there was a very long silence.

At last someone spoke. "But it isn't about the Queen."

"Yes it is. It's metaphorical."

This explanation caused a further silence. Several of the members of the Grand Council looked from one to the other to see if anyone knew what *metaphorical* meant.

"Well, I'm sure it's very profound," an elder drone said doubtfully.

"Personally I think it's a lot of rubbish," declared a burly drone called Guy who, though not actually a member of the Council, had been appointed its usher on account of his magnificent physique. Since his appointment he had strutted about, flexing his mandibles and bullying lesser bees. He sneered at the conversation of more intellectual young drones and was dismissive of their fragile hopes and dreams. "Where's the common sense in all this?" he liked to ask, "I'm a practical bee, I believe in common sense."

Mo and Alfred disliked Guy. They suspected that what he called common sense was what most bees would call stupidity but did not say so out loud because Guy knew a lot of important drones.

Now Alfred ignored Guy's comment. It was not worth answering. What would Guy know about poetry? He was nothing but a muscle-bound chitin-head.

Guy misunderstood his silence. "Metaphorical twaddle," he sneered.

He had gone too far. Alfred alighted on the threshold and raised his two front legs in an aggressive stance. "Don't you know what a metaphor is?" he challenged.

"No, and I don't want to." Guy ignored

Alfred's aggressive stance and continued to hover in the air.

"Only a fool takes pride in being ignorant," Alfred shouted.

It was a matter of honor now. Guy alighted on the threshold and raised his front legs in answer to Alfred's insult. "Who are you calling a fool?" he asked in a nasty tone.

"You've chosen to be a fool, haven't you?"

"Now, now," an elder drone said soothingly, alighting between them to keep the peace, "suppose we let Alfred explain his poem himself." He turned to Alfred. "You said it was meta . . . meta . . . er . . ."

"Metaphorical," Alfred said again. He allowed himself to be calmed and stood on all six legs again. He turned away from Guy and flew up to address the Council. "The willow is a metaphor for the Queen," he explained, "she's important, like the first honey."

"Why do you say the Queen is floating on the breeze?" somebody asked.

"That's not the Queen. She's not floating on the breeze. The willow seed is."

It was true. All day downy seeds had drifted across the orchard from the willow that overhung the riverbank. Even now they floated, fluffy and white, above the threshold board. The drones looked up and nodded wisely. The poem was telling the truth.

"What has that to do with the Queen then?" Guy asked, still trying to find something to criticize.

"It's meant to convey the sense of loss. Our Queen has gone away forever." Alfred's voice broke and he bowed his head.

"It's all perfectly obvious," Mo agreed in a loud voice. He didn't think it was obvious at all but he could see that his friend Alfred was deeply moved.

There was another long silence. The drones looked uneasily from one to another. Alfred's poem was a little odd but he had managed to voice the unspoken anxiety of each.

"Do you think the Queen will ever come back?" asked a young drone, who had hatched on the day that the swarm left and did not remember the old Queen.

"No, she has gone forever," the Grand Drone answered solemnly.

"What will we do without her?"

"We must wait for a sign," the Grand Drone looked upward. The sun shone brightly. The sky was blue. "Somewhere up there," he said in a reverent voice, "the Great Drone is watching. He sees our loss, our pain. Soon He will give us a sign. The Great Drone in the Sky watches over all of His drones."

Alfred and Mo fixed their compound eyes on the upper blue and when the drones rose in a great humming mass and hovered high above the orchard, praising with one voice the Great Drone in the Sky, Alfred flew up and joined in with tremulous hope in his heart. Mo was left alone, absorbed in anguished meditation. "Why?" he asked, scanning the wide, empty blue for a sign. "Why?" The sky gave no sign of an answer.

Above an old plum tree the massed drones wheeled upward and then swooped down again. Mo, despairing of an answer to his profound question, flew up among them. The Grand Drone began to intone the praises of the Great

Drone. Two by two, the drones formed a long file behind him and followed him down to the hive.

The Grand Drone was first to alight. He led the procession inside. The others followed devoutly, obstructing, for a time, the passage of field bees carrying home their harvest of pollen and honey.

"Giver of nectar," the Grand Drone chanted.

"Grant us honey," the drones echoed in unison.

"Light in the sky . . ."

"Dew on the petal . . ."

"Summer shower . . ."

"Great Giver of all . . ."

"Grant us honey . . ."

"Great Drone in the Sky . . ."

"Great Drone, Father of all."

They crowded into the passageways and passed into the brood chamber where the brood were still being tended by workers. They proceeded across the comb, dislodging workers who were tidying and polishing used cells, in readiness for the future. Then the procession turned a corner and entered the passageway that passed between the frames of stored honey at the back of the hive.

Here the litany came to an end. The Grand Drone ceremoniously uncapped a honey cell and drank in celebration of the GDS. The rest of the drones quickly joined in the ceremony and gorged on honey till they were filled. Then, the ceremony at an end, they lurched and stumbled to the warmest part of the brood comb, which was where they liked to sleep.

in the evenings the hive was
cooler. Even when the field bees came home at
night, there were no longer enough bees to create the sort of intense heat that had been there
when the hive had a full colony. Before the
departure of the Queen, fanning continued day

and night. At that time the hive was so crowded that hundreds of bees slept in clusters on the outside walls of the hive because there was no room for them inside. Now, not so many bees were needed to fan.

When rain fell on the fourth evening after the departure of the swarm, the air outside was cool and still. Thora was relieved of fanning just before nightfall. Exhausted, she slept deeply but sensed, in her sleep, the thump of gusting wind and storm against the sides of the hive. In the morning nobody stirred from the cluster. The air had grown almost as chill as winter. Squalls of rain rattled intermittently on the roof, making the whole hive tremble. The bees clung together for warmth, sharing their body heat with the brood. All day they stayed in the cluster. The usual routine of work came to a standstill and they did not even take cleansing flights. As night fell a mouse, flooded out of his nest by the downpour, crept inside to shelter in the warmth of the hive. There were no guards at the entrance to stop him.

The summer storm ended as abruptly as it

began. Day was dawning when Thora was roused out of her sleep by a song that she had never heard before. It was a high-pitched, furious sound. She started awake, all her senses alert. The song warned of danger, an intruder, an enemy. It was a song of battle, a summons to defend the hive. She joined the throng that already hastened along the middle passageways. The enemy had penetrated deep into the hive, to the brood chamber itself, with its precious brood. Angrily, Thora pushed and butted her way through the thrashing mass of bees that crushed her on all sides. She saw that a comb had been ripped and torn and part of the brood destroyed. Then she saw the enemy, a large, fur-covered brute with fierce teeth and an alien smell. She heard the war cry "Mouse!" and the song of battle raged even louder.

At first the mouse snapped back at the attacking bees. Then, realizing there were too many of them, he turned to flee. He darted along a passageway, searching for an exit. There was no escape. Bees came from all sides and swarmed over him.

They tried to drive their stingers into his body but found that they could not penetrate the dense fur. Ruthlessly they clung to him, searching with their sting feelers for a place which they could sting. At last the mouse uttered a high-pitched screech. A bee had crawled underneath his tail and found a hairless part.

Other bees rushed to attack the undefended place. The mouse shrieked in terror. Thora, driven by rage, pushed and jostled. More than anything she wanted to come close and drive her sting into the writhing, screaming enemy.

For a while his agony sounded loudly above the raging song of the bees. Then, poisoned by the venom of a hundred stings, he cried more faintly till in the end he only twitched and lay still. Abruptly, the bees ended their song of battle and went back to work.

The floor of the hive was littered with dead and dying bees who had used their stings to destroy the enemy. Unable to withdraw the barbs, they had wrenched them from their bodies, inflicting fatal injury on themselves. As well as dead bees, there were half-eaten larvae and immature pupae which had been tossed by the mouse from their cells.

"Can you help me?" Belle asked Thora when she was unable to drag an outsized drone pupa outside by herself. Thora helped her tug the corpse to the hive entrance. Then they went on working together. Thora was pleased to have made a friend. A lot of the time worker bees were too busy to stop for conversation, but Belle chattered all the time while she worked.

She and Thora gathered dead bees and carried them outside. The early sun shone on the east side of the hive, and dew lay heavily on the blades of grass beneath. Drones were already hovering about the threshold, although they did not usually go outside till afternoon. Today they were drawn out earlier than usual by the heat of the early sun and by the excitement of repeating over and over the story of the mouse. Thora and Belle did not stay to enjoy the sunlight. There was work to be done.

All morning they cleaned and tidied. One half-matured drone pupa kicked violently when they tried to carry him and fought against being thrown outside. Thora hesitated and let go of his stumpy legs. "Do you think he will live?" she asked doubtfully.

"He's no good for anything," Belle said, tugging him along by the wings.

"Ouch, let go," cried the pupa. He kicked again and wriggled free of Belle's grip.

"You have to go outside," Belle insisted. The pupa was bedraggled and undersized. Now that he was out of his capped cell he could never grow to be a proper drone.

"But I'm hungry," he said, and extended his tongue as far as it would go.

It was hard to resist a request for food. Thora, without even thinking, regurgitated some bee milk and let him take it from her tongue. She felt a little sorry for him. "Let's give him a chance," she said, starting to clean him up.

"We really shouldn't," Belle argued. However, she helped Thora lick the immature drone all over till he was clean and his sparse body hair fluffy. Then they fed him again and put him back on the brood comb where he would be warm.

"What's your name?" Belle asked, but he looked bewildered and shook his head.

"We'll call you Daisy," Thora said, "would you like that?"

He nodded his head vigorously. Contentedly he settled down on the brood comb to sleep.

Thora and Belle worked till all the dead bees were disposed of. While they were cleaning up, other bees had filled their sacs with honey and clustered together to secrete wax. Now their wax was ready and they went to work to repair the damaged brood combs. Thora considered going with them to work at chewing and molding wax, but Belle insisted that she stay and help dispose of the mouse.

The corpse was still in the corner where he had sought refuge from the bees. It was too heavy to be moved and carried outside but could not be left. Decaying flesh would foul the hive.

"There's only one way," Belle decided, "we'll have to strip it down." Other workers came to help. It took two days to strip the mouse until only white, clean-picked bones remained. The bones were too heavy to be carried outside and too hard to be gnawed into small pieces.

"We need propolis," Belle announced and sent a young house bee to tell the field bees. The mouse's bones would have to be embalmed in a mixture of resin and wax, sealed away forever so that they would not pollute the hive.

For a whole day a steady stream of field bees carried propolis from a cluster of Norway spruce that grew near the north end of the orchard. Normally propolis was used to repair cracks or damaged places in the hive and to secure the honey frames. Now the field bees carried the sticky resin to the young house bees waiting inside the hive entrance, who in turn brought it to Belle.

"Is the wax ready?" Belle asked a group of bees who had been clustering nearby. They had been there for hours, patiently secreting wax.

"Here you are," they said, tumbling eagerly out of the cluster and passing the wax in small, fine platelets to the crowd of workers who were embalming the mouse.

It took hours to mix the propolis with wax. It had to be kneaded and pounded and then placed layer upon layer over the white bones till they were securely sealed against the wall of the hive.

It was evening before the workers finished the task and went outside to make a routine cleansing flight. On their way back they accepted a meal of regurgitated honey from a couple of house bees, and begged some freshly harvested pollen from a field bee who was glad to unload her pollen baskets. After feeding they crawled deep into the hive and clustered with other tired worker bees in the brood chamber.

Outside the sun was setting. A shaft of evening light shone through a crack in the old, weathered timber of the hive and fell on the spread-eagled skeleton of the mouse. It glowed amber but nobody paid any attention. The bees were listening, not looking. A new sound rang out in the hive. It was a sound that made every worker bee catch her breath and listen. Thora and Belle stirred and forgot how tired they were.

The sound was coming from beside them, right in the brood chamber. It was a faint, high-pitched piping, and its source was a large, cup-shaped brood cell that hung vertically from the brood comb.

As the bees listened, they grew serene. They hummed a song of joy. The voice that sang clear and loud from the brood chamber was the voice of a young, virgin Queen.

outside, summer twilight lingered. A
few field bees, who had been foraging far away,
were still coming home. They could be heard
alighting with a plop on the threshold, heavy
with the weight of nectar and pollen. As they
unburdened themselves and let young hive

workers carry their harvest inside, they paused and listened too. They heard the song of the young Queen and lifted their voices in the song of joy.

Thora and Belle moved aside to let the late workers carry pollen into the brood comb and butt it into cells with their heads. They were too excited now to sleep. Again and again they heard the Queen sing her song. After the first tentative notes it grew louder. Now she jeered and insulted at the top of her voice. She dared any other Queen to match her, to equal her beauty, her intelligence, her fecundity.

The drones were sleeping heavily in the center of the brood and were slow to waken. Most of them had spent the evening drinking honey and were rowdy and drunk before they fell asleep. Now, however, they stirred sleepily and listened.

"Whoa," said Guy, who had been less drunk than the others, "do you hear what I hear?"

Alfred roused himself from his evening stupor. He felt a brief flicker of desire. Drowsily he tried to gather his thoughts. Desire for what? Not more honey. He was sated with honey. He couldn't possibly drink any more tonight. What he desired was something more sublime. Vaguely, he wondered what could possibly be more sublime than honey.

"A Queen, it's the song of a Queen," cried out the puny drone called Daisy. "A Queen for a drone. A drone for a Queen. Who will be the one? Who will die for love of his Queen?" Over and over he babbled meaninglessly, and his shrill voice echoed strangely among the honeycombs suspended overhead.

Alfred shook himself awake. What did Daisy think he was doing, wailing in the middle of the night, wakening up other drones? Sometimes Daisy could be an utter nuisance.

"Do be quiet, Daisy," Alfred said with a yawn, but Daisy went on noisily.

Properly speaking, Daisy wasn't a drone at all. Some silly workers had neglected to throw him out when he was torn, prematurely, from his pupa cell. He ought to have been discarded then, along with the rest of the refuse and broken combs. He just didn't belong. Daisy was defective, not fully drone. Not only was his body undersized and immature, but his mind also seemed not quite complete.

The song of the Queen sounded again. Alfred started. "Great Drone," he gasped. There was a shred of meaning, this time, in Daisy's babble. He listened intently and remembered what it was that was more sublime than honey. His destiny was beckoning, his *destiny*, which had nothing to do with honey. His destiny was something infinitely higher, the future of the hive.

He felt the stirring of passion. His Queen was somewhere near. He heard her song. She was offering, in a shrill voice, to fight any other Queen in the hive. So sweet. Sweeter than the sweetest honey, lovelier than sunshine. "My Queen," he murmured blissfully to himself, but Guy overheard.

"What do you mean, *your* Queen?" he challenged unpleasantly. Guy had been waiting for this moment. Even when the hive had no Queen, he had been preparing himself. He kept himself fit by flying out whenever it was sunny in quest of innocent young virgin Queens who might be tempted by his husky physique. He told tall tales about his prowess as a lover and boasted of how he could fly six miles without alighting.

"Well, she belongs to all of us, doesn't she," Alfred reasoned, rubbing sleep from the hexagonal lenses of his compound eyes.

"Exactly, she belongs to all of us," Mo agreed. "The Queen can choose whichever one of us she pleases."

"You just watch it," Guy threatened.

"Oh yes?" Alfred retorted with as much menace as he could muster.

"Oh yes."

"Now, now, let the best drone win," the Grand Drone said soothingly when he noticed that several groups of drones were breaking into unseemly argument. "Of course," he murmured to himself as the hubbub died down, "a Grand Drone is practically a king. A fit mate for a Queen, I should think."

Mo heard him. "All's fair in love and war," he muttered under his breath. It sounded subversive but then, a lot of what he said and thought seemed subversive, even to himself.

He liked being the rebel of the hive. Thinking radical thoughts was exciting. It was very agreeable to question the myths that other drones mistook for truth. Besides, someone had to question things. Somebody had to debunk all the silly accepted ideas that could accumulate in an old hive. Mo was the only drone who weighed everything, criticized everything, and probed deep into the mysteries of existence. When drones like Guy were flying miles in a mindless search for Queens, Mo could be found on the east corner of the alighting board, pacing backward and forward, thinking profound, radical thoughts and occasionally even voicing them to other intellectual young drones.

Alfred was also one of the set who hovered around the east corner. Flying six miles in quest of virgin Queens was a bit too energetic for a poet. What he most liked to do on sunny afternoons was hover above the threshold and dream.

On the whole, it was easier to dream about Queens than to fly in quest of them. Guy and his friends never actually found Queens anyway. They buzzed around in drone congregation areas miles from home, telling tall tales about nuptial flights they had been on and of virgin Queens who had loved them. It was all rubbish. None of them had ever gotten close to a Queen. They only dreamed about it.

"None of you has ever had a Queen," Daisy would jeer at them in his odd, squeaky voice. "Dead drones don't tell."

in the morning the unhatched
Queen sang again, and a sister Queen answered
her challenge from another Queen cell. Workers
helped thin the capping of the first Queen's cell.
She herself worked on the inside to cut the capping neatly, three quarters of the way around,

leaving the last quarter to act as a hinge when she lifted the cap.

"Ah!" the workers gasped with delight as she emerged. She was long-bodied, graceful, beautiful. They surrounded her, humming joyfully. They cleaned her, licking her all over from the tips of her antennae to the end of her abdomen. Several pushed forward to offer regurgitated bee milk. The Queen delicately sipped their offerings with the extended tip of her tongue.

Suddenly she paused and listened. A thin piping arose from somewhere in the brood chamber. Workers ignored the new piping and went on paying court to their Queen, fondling her head, touching their antennae to hers, and stroking her wings. The Queen rose, standing on four legs with her front legs raised, and hummed a song of anger. She would not tolerate a rival in the hive.

She was not to be soothed with affection. "Out of my way," she said, pushing the eager workers aside. She raised her voice in the battle challenge of the Queen. Her attendants hurried after as she rushed across the comb to the Queen cell where her rival made a defiant reply. Fiercely she tore open the comb and before her rival could emerge, stung her to death.

"Are there more?" she demanded. The workers led her to two other Queen cells where younger, immature Queens had not yet answered the royal challenge. They helped her tear the waxen walls apart and stood aside to let her sting each of the Queens to death. Only a Queen might kill another Queen.

Satisfied that there were no more rivals in the hive, the Queen turned her attention once more to the bee milk that her attendants offered her. "Mmm," she murmured, and they gave her more. When she finished feeding, she peered into the surrounding darkness. "This is all mine?"

"Yes, Your Majesty, it's all yours," said a young bee who had assumed the role of chief attendant.

"Let's look around," the Queen said. Shedding her royal dignity, she gleefully scampered across the comb. The attendants who had been standing in front of her moved respectfully backward and found themselves hanging upside-down on the edge of the frame as she eagerly climbed over them. They hastily righted themselves and hurried after her.

The young Queen examined her domain. There were the remaining brood cells where pupating workers were almost ready to emerge as mature bees. There were drone broods which would take several days longer. There were stores of honey and pollen. Bees came and went, laboring eagerly and enthusiastically, ecstatic in the knowledge that they had a Queen.

"Aren't there any mature drones?" the Queen asked when she had inspected the drone broods with their high-domed cappings.

"Yes, Your Majesty," said one attendant.

"Where are they?"

"Around and about. Here and there."

"I don't see any."

The attendant bee changed the subject. The Queen would not be ready to mate for another four days at least. Meanwhile, she would have to be protected. "Look, Your Majesty, here is where we store pollen. See this yellow dandelion pollen, it was gathered in March."

The Queen looked and listened, eager to learn. Worker bees crowded around, delighted to show her the wonders of the hive.

Belle and Thora were among the lucky ones. They were right beside the Queen cell when she emerged, and Belle was the first worker to push forward and offer her regurgitated food. "I can't believe I was the first," she said again and again.

"I got to clean one of her antennae," Thora said contentedly. She did not envy Belle. A bee could smell and taste and feel with her antennae. She had experienced the new Queen just as fully as Belle.

after the first day, the virgin Queen
moved freely around the hive, unhampered by
too much attention from workers. That would
come later. For now it was enough to be aware of
her radiant presence.

However she still needed care. She had to be fed and groomed. She needed protection from idiotic drones who kept Queen-questing around the hive now that they knew there was a virgin Queen somewhere inside.

While the workers avoided interfering too much with her explorations, they gladly answered her questions and discreetly kept drones at a distance. One morning, just before noon, a bunch of noisy, half-drunken drones blundered past, shouting obscenities. Thora and some other workers unobtrusively steered the Queen away to the other side of the brood chamber, out of their path.

"Make way, make way," the Grand Drone shouted importantly.

"Scrubbers," Guy snorted contemptuously, "they get everywhere. Do keep these passageways clear. Can't you see we're on important business?"

He made the mistake of bumping into Belle who was carrying old wax and debris from the combs. "Now look what you've done," she exclaimed, when the litter was knocked from her mandibles. "Can't you drones look where you're going?"

"Since when have cleaning bees presumed to give orders to drones?" Guy asked loftily.

"Since when have drones become lords of the hive?" Belle retorted.

"Scrubbers," Daisy jeered, and hid behind Guy.

"We are the royal consorts," Guy said importantly, "we are the destiny of the hive. You should show more respect."

"You? The destiny of the hive?" Belle exclaimed. "Do you seriously think the destiny of the hive depends on a lot of fat, useless, lazy, drunken drones?" She glared fiercely at him. "Get out of my way," she snapped. Startled, Guy let himself be pushed aside.

"Scrubbers," Daisy shouted, and hid behind Guy again.

Belle recognized the immature drone whom she had saved from being thrown out. "Hey you!" she called.

"Me?"

"Aren't you Daisy?"

"That's me."

"You're that lump of rubbish I forgot to throw out. I'd better do it now." She darted toward him.

Daisy dashed away. "Yah," he jeered when he thought he was at a safe distance. Then, remembering his importance as a drone, he pushed his way through a group of workers who were mending the caps on some honey cells and kicked a hole in one of the cappings as he passed.

Alfred, coming behind everybody else, tried to make amends. "Ever so sorry for barging in like this," he apologized.

"Oh, go away," several workers exclaimed.

"But we're looking for our Queen," Alfred explained politely. "It's terribly important that we should find her." He toddled along the comb in the direction the other drones had taken. The drones had all passed by without realizing that their Queen was only inches away.

"What was all that?" the Queen asked, intrigued by the commotion.

"Drones, Your Majesty," Belle replied. She

bowed low to show how deeply honored she was at being spoken to by the Queen.

"Drones?" the Queen exclaimed. "Where?"

"They're gone now," Belle said, "you don't have to worry about them."

"Worry about them? But I'm just dying to meet them," the Queen said with a silly giggle.

An elder worker shook her head and tutted gravely. "Not yet, Your Majesty, not yet."

The drones had satisfied themselves that their Queen was not inside the hive. They gathered outside in rowdy groups and hung about the threshold for over an hour, talking loudly and animatedly about where she might be. They jostled field bees coming in with water to cool the hive. They demanded nectar from workers who came with full nectar sacs. They snatched a pollen pellet from the leg basket of an incoming worker and kicked it up and down the threshold, cheering excitedly. Then, while the sun was still directly overhead, they suddenly remembered their Queen. They flew up in the air and with a loud humming went off in quest of her.

the workers were industriously preparing for the future now. All day the hive
echoed with their contented humming. The cell
builders worked at drawing out still more waxen
cells, filling them with nectar, and preparing the

brood chamber for a new brood which would replace the numbers lost to the swarm.

Thora and Belle found they were kept busy. Sometimes they waited near the entrance to collect nectar and pollen from foraging bees and carry it into the hive for storage in the combs. At other times they helped store it. Pollen was packed in the combs in front of the brood chamber, nectar at the back. Pollen had also to be stored in cells on the outer edges of the brood comb so that very young, newly emerged workers would have easy access to it. It would be an important food for the very young bees, who would secrete bee milk and act as nursemaids to the future brood.

Thora and Belle had one favorite job: fetching and carrying for the Queen. Officially workers were not supposed to pay court to a virgin Queen. However she was so beautiful and received their attentions so graciously that they took every opportunity they could to tend her. The Queen substance that she secreted would not be real Queen substance until she mated, but even so, it was much nicer than having no

Queen substance at all. The worker bees absorbed it, touching their Queen and licking her. Then they passed it along from one to another, and even gave some to drones who hummed with excitement when they realized what it was and dashed away eagerly to try yet again to find their virgin Queen.

The weather continued fine. Outside the air was warm, but inside the hive the temperature was now regulated by more recently hatched bees who had to fan incessantly, just as Thora used to do. They, too, fanned on the edge of the honeycombs, evaporating the nectar till it became ripe honey ready for capping with wax. Dozens of bees hovered outside on the threshold, fanning out the warm air of the hive and circulating its scent into the air.

On sunny afternoons the Grand Council of Drones convened above the threshold for many lengthy sessions. There were weighty matters to be dealt with. It was agreed that things had been allowed to go along for too long in any old haphazard way. The previous Council had been

remiss in not ordering matters of public importance in a proper fashion.

"We must first concern ourselves with the
regulation of the sun," one long-winded drone
declared, and after he had spoken for ten minutes on the subject the council voted unanimously to promulgate proper sunlight laws. It
was ordered, by decree of the Grand Council,
that the sun was to rise at dawn and set at dusk.
Any other arrangement would not be permitted.
An officer would be appointed to ensure that the
decree was enforced. Mo suddenly found himself
elevated to the position of Inspector of Sunlight.
He was dubious. "What do you think?" he asked
Alfred.

"Well, it's better than not having any job at
all, isn't it?"

"It will mean getting up early," Mo said, feeling already the burden of responsibility.

"And going to bed late too," he added with
dismay. However, it was, as Alfred said, better
than having no position. Anything was better
than being a nobody.

Other motions also were moved and voted upon. A committee was set up to supervise the construction of honey storage cells and to examine alternatives to the hexagonal cell shape traditionally used.

"Six-sided cells are all very well," explained a drone who had a reputation for higher mathematical thinking, "but there are alternatives. I believe we should think bigger — why not eight sides or nine or even ten? Think how much more honey could be stored!"

This grandiose proposal was received with a tremendous burst of enthusiastic applause, and a suitably qualified committee of drones was appointed to examine the matter.

when the queen was three days old, she found the hive entrance and stood looking in astonishment at the bright beam of midday sun that shone through the narrow aperture.

"What is it?" she asked.

"Sunlight, Your Majesty," Belle replied. She had paused in her work to offer food to the Queen and to stroke her body as she passed.

"And what is that sound?"

"What sound, Your Majesty?"

"That whirring? Are there bees out there?"

"Those are the wings of bees. The scent of the hive is being fanned into the air so that field bees can find their way home."

"If I went outside, would I find my way home?"

It was the question the workers had been dreading. Sooner or later the Queen would want to leave the hive. She would have to learn to spread her wings, to fly, to mate, and to find her way home again. Upon her nuptial flight depended the future of the hive, yet every moment out of the hive would be fraught with danger. If she were lost or snatched by a foraging bird the hive too would die. Without a Queen there could be no future. Belle, deliberating upon the dangers, hesitated to give an answer.

"Well, could I find my way home?" the Queen asked impatiently.

"Yes, I think you could, so long as you don't go too far at first," Thora said gravely.

The Queen approached the entrance and examined it carefully. Some field bees coming in laden with nectar stopped to watch. The Queen hesitated and drew back. Belle and Thora relaxed. Perhaps she would not fly today.

"But it's perfectly safe," a field bee urged. "It's midday now. Birds mostly feed in the morning and the evening. There is very little danger from them now."

The Queen moved forward again, went all the way to the threshold, and started back with a small cry. "It's so bright out there!"

"That is sunlight," the field bee explained, "you'll soon get used to it."

The Queen moved forward, then hesitated once more. "Go on," the field bee urged.

She edged forward cautiously all the way to the threshold of the hive. Hive bees followed and crowded anxiously around her. She felt the warmth of the sun on her wings and with her lovely compound eyes, composed of five thousand hexagonal lenses, she saw light and color all around.

"But it's beautiful" she exclaimed. Slowly she spread her wings and rose, humming, from the threshold. She flew upward, flying in a circle but keeping close to the hive. Thora and Belle watched anxiously, poised to attack any enemy that might approach.

The drones, high above, hovered excitedly.

"Kwagh!" Guy groaned appreciatively. "Just look at that!"

The young Queen flew in wider and wider circles around the hive. The drones hummed loudly, trying to attract her attention.

"Look at those antennae!" one of Guy's cronies called loudly, trying hard to be noticed.

"Kwagh," Guy groaned again.

"And that abdomen!"

"Kwa-a-gh!"

"Those cute little mandibles!"

"Kwa-a-a-a-gh!"

Alfred didn't join in. He didn't even fly up to hover with the other drones. He was deeply shamed by their loudmouthed remarks and wished he could do something to show the Queen that not all drones were like Guy and his friends.

He remained near the threshold in the hope of being close to her when she alighted again.

He longed to come near enough to smell her scent, to admire the lovely, shaded stripes of her long, slender abdomen, to hear the whirr of her wings and the sound of her voice. He was not like those other drones. He wanted her to know that.

His love was pure and idealistic. He loved the beauty of his Queen but even more he loved her noble spirit. He didn't actually have any reason yet to suppose that the Queen had a noble spirit but equally he had no reason to suppose that she did not. Surely a Queen would exist on a sublime, lofty plane, far above those unattractive little worker females whose minds were earthbound, limited by the physical needs of the hive and the brood. It was only natural that she would.

He alone understood her grace and loveliness,

he alone divined her wit and intelligence. He had never had a conversation with her and was not personally acquainted with anyone who had, but he knew that if he did have the chance to speak to her, she would share his delight in the mysteries of the earth and the sun and the sky. She would share his appreciation of what was rare and beautiful. She would understand his poetry.

If, like a worker bee, he could bear gifts, he would bring honey to his Queen. He would bring her the most delectable reserves of first spring honey. Alas, he was a drone. He could offer only his dronehood and that was a paltry gift which any drone could give. Except Daisy, perhaps.

He could almost have wished that nature had endowed him, like workers, with the humble capacity to harvest honey and pollen, to secrete wax, to build and shape waxen cells. All he could create was poetry. And since his poetry was the only gift he had to give, she would have that. He would make her a poem.

When the Queen alighted on the threshold he

was overwhelmed with delight. He hurried to be close to her only to be pushed away by her attendants. "My Queen," he called out, "my Queen!"

The Queen paused and looked around. "Did someone call?"

"No one of any importance," a worker bee said crossly, and nudged the Queen toward the hive entrance.

The Queen caught sight of Alfred. "Ooh, it's a drone," she exclaimed and turned to look at him more closely. "What's your name?"

Alfred struggled for words. None came. "I . . . I . . . I . . ." he stammered in an agony of suppressed passion. Suddenly he remembered he should bow. He bowed deeply.

"Isn't he charming?" the Queen said with a giggle.

Alfred tried to speak but still no words would come. He was covered with confusion. He nodded his head from side to side and stamped his legs.

The Queen laughed delightedly. "What a

funny fellow," she exclaimed. "Are all drones so clumsy and funny and fat?"

"Of course not," said the attendant worker who had spoken before. She scowled fiercely at Alfred. Then she turned away and succeeded, with the help of the other hive bees, in steering the Queen to the entrance and inside the hive.

Alfred was devastated. Why had he not spoken? The Queen had noticed him, encouraged him to speak and he had been tongue-tied. Why had he performed that idiotic dance and made himself look a fool? He banged his head on the alighting board in his frustration. How could he have made such a mess of things?

"Did you see the Queen?" Mo said, flying down and alighting beside him.

"Yes," Alfred groaned.

"What's wrong with you?"

Alfred struck his head on the board again and again.

"Hey—Hey! Take it easy," Mo protested. "Things can't be that bad."

"They are."

"What's the matter?"

"I had the chance to speak to her and I couldn't."

"Who?"

"The Queen. She spoke to me."

"The Queen spoke to you?" Mo was incredulous. Alfred wasn't exactly handsome. More the honey-swilling, slob type.

"I couldn't say a word. What's wrong with me?"

"Wrong? Why should anything be wrong? You're the luckiest drone in the hive. You've been close enough to the Queen for her to speak to you. What did she say?"

Maybe it wasn't so bad after all, Alfred consoled himself. After all, she had wanted to speak to him. He had caught her eye. She had stopped and looked at him. Her first impression of him was that he was charming. She did say charming.

And then, he remembered with intense humiliation that she also said he was clumsy and fat and funny. Tomorrow, first thing tomorrow, he would fly away from the hive and get fit. Guy could fly six miles without alighting. It was just a matter of practice. He would fly out to the fields first thing in the morning and get really fit.

And he would take less honey. He would fast from honey for the rest of the day. He was drinking far too much honey. It couldn't be good for him to be drunk every night. He would stop bingeing on honey and eat pollen instead. Pollen was good for building muscle. He would take lots of pollen and exercise. Then the Queen wouldn't think he was fat.

"Well? What did she say?"

"She asked me my name, that's all." Alfred couldn't bring himself to tell Mo the rest.

11

two days of rain followed. The bees remained inside, listening to raindrops pattering on the roof. Even though the worker bees could no longer harvest outdoors, there was much to be done inside, cleaning the combs, mopping up after the drones, caring for the Queen. Even when they weren't doing any active work they could work at making wax.

On the first day of rain Belle and Thora filled their stomachs with honey and spent most of the day clustered with other bees, secreting wax in their wax glands on the front of their abdomens and using it to build comb. Toward evening, however, they sat on the brood with the drones because there was no more work to be done, for the moment at least.

Thora nodded in recognition at Alfred. He was puzzled. "Do I know you?"

"I'm Thora. You invited me to uncap some honey with you on swarming day. Don't you remember?"

"I'm afraid not."

"And you got disgustingly drunk. I had to clean you down," Belle added.

"Naughty me," he said, pleased that he had made an impression on the little worker bees.

"What's your name then?"

Thora introduced Belle and Alfred introduced Mo. "I'm Poet Laureate," he announced importantly, "and Mo is Inspector of Sunlight."

"What does a poet do?" Thora asked with interest.

"I have sublime thoughts and feelings, which I express in sublime poems."

"And what does an Inspector of Sunlight do?" Belle asked.

"I . . . er, I regulate the motions of the sun," Mo explained.

"The sun? You regulate the sun?" Belle was awed at Mo's immense power.

"Well actually, I've just been appointed to the job. I haven't taken up my duties yet. As a matter of fact, you could oblige me. I have to get up early to check that the ordinance of the Council is being properly observed. Perhaps you would be kind enough to call me in the morning?"

"Yes, of course," Belle said eagerly, pleased to be given such an important task.

"What do you work at?" Alfred asked, turning to Thora.

"Oh, this and that," she replied, a little bit ashamed to admit that she did nothing more exciting than cleaning the hive and building wax cells when Alfred was composing sublime poetry and Mo was regulating the sun.

"We're workers, house bees. We work in the hive. That's all," Belle said bluntly.

"I'm afraid we lead very uninteresting lives." Thora was apologetic.

"What do you workers do with your lives when you're not working?" Mo asked. "What are your dreams, your ambitions?"

"Dreams?" Thora was bewildered.

"Workers don't dream," Belle explained. "When we sleep we are tired. We don't dream."

"That's not what I mean," Mo explained patiently. "I don't mean what you dream when you're asleep. What I want to know is what you think about when you're not thinking about your work?"

"What else is there to think about?" Belle asked. "The hive is our whole existence. We're born to work."

"That's all? You work and then you die? Is there nothing else in your existence?" Mo felt a profound pity for the wretched little workers whose world was such a small place.

"What else could there be?"

"Don't you ever want to be free?"

Belle shook her head.

"Don't you ever want to fly out of the hive just to look at things?"

"Look at what?"

"Flowers, trees, the earth. Don't you ever want just a little time, a little space in which you can be yourself?" Mo spoke with passion. How terrible that these little workers didn't know how to be free.

"But without the hive we're nothing," Thora ventured timidly.

"That's not true." Mo felt a missionary zeal. Together, he and Alfred could show these workers the way to a better life. "We're all individuals," he explained, "we're born free. We can choose. You don't have to be the slave of the hive."

"But we choose to work," Belle insisted.

"No, you've been conditioned to think that you must clean the hive and build combs and nurture the young and harvest nectar and pollen. From the moment you were born you have worked, and nobody has ever told you that you could do anything else. But you don't have to. You can choose not to."

"Yes," Alfred agreed enthusiastically, "you can choose not to."

"What would we do instead?" Thora asked.

"You could improve your mind. Widen your horizons. Go and see the rest of the world. There's more to life than the darkness of the hive," Mo said with enthusiasm.

"Go outside, be free," Alfred urged.

Thora stayed awake a long time that night thinking about what Mo and Alfred had said. It was terrifying talk. The idea of existing without the hive appalled her. And yet, to be free, to choose. Those words created a yearning for something that she could hardly imagine. To be free. Free of the hive. Free of her destiny as a worker.

After all, what was there in life for a worker, what reward when her work was done? It was just as they said, workers worked from the moment they were born till they died. If she continued her life as a worker bee she would never

do anything but serve the hive, working incessantly till she grew too old to work. Then she
would die.

She had seen old female bees who worked till
their wings grew ragged and they could fly no
more. Some dropped to the ground when their
flight fell short of the threshold board. They fell,
still laden with their harvest, and were sliced in
half and carried away by predatory wasps who
hung about waiting for such an opportunity. A
meal for a wasp, what a horrible way to die.
Other workers died far away from the hive, too
exhausted to come home.

Sometimes an old worker bee, her wings
ragged and torn with use, lingered a few days in
the hive before she died. Thora knew to ignore
such a bee and to disregard her requests for food.
It was kinder. She had served her purpose and
the hive had no further use for her. It was the
destiny of a worker to work herself to death for
the good of the hive. Until now Thora had taken
it for granted. What else was there for a worker
to do?

Mo and Alfred disturbed those certainties.

They had told her she could choose. She fretted and worried for a long time, twisting and turning, disturbing other workers who were sleeping close to her in the warm nighttime cluster. Eventually she fell asleep and dreamed that she flew outside into the sunlight, gorged herself on nectar, and lay in the heart of a wild white rose under the noonday sun. A loud downpour of rain drumming on the roof of the hive wakened her out of her dream. She nudged Belle awake. "I had a dream."

"A dream? Don't be silly."

"But I did."

"You've been listening too long to those stupid drones," Belle scolded. "Workers don't have dreams. We just work."

"But I did have a dream."

"Nonsense. Go back to sleep."

In the morning it was still raining. Belle wriggled into the center of the cluster to call Mo, but he didn't think it worthwhile getting up. He couldn't inspect the sunrise while it was raining outside.

When Belle and Thora were working

together that day, Thora wanted to talk about her dream but Belle wouldn't listen.

"I'll go and tell Mo and Alfred," she said indignantly, "they'll listen."

Mo and Alfred were enormously impressed. "You see," Mo said triumphantly, "you're broadening your horizons already. You're probably the only worker in the hive who has had a dream about not working."

"It was such a strange feeling," Thora said, trying to find words for it, "as if nothing in the world mattered except lying among those petals, looking at the sky."

"It's called being idle," Mo explained.

"Idle?"

"You've been dreaming you were idle."

"Have you ever been idle?" Alfred asked interestedly.

"No."

"Then you've just made a wonderful imaginative leap. You have experienced idleness in your dream."

"So that's what it was? Idleness?"

"Yes. Did you enjoy being idle?"

"It was such an odd feeling. Having no care, no responsibility."

Mo turned to Alfred. "Isn't that marvelous? She's really grasped the concept of idleness."

"Keep dreaming, you have a talent for it," Alfred said encouragingly.

He and Mo were quite enthusiastic about the idea of liberating the workers. It would be such a worthwhile thing to improve their little minds and the quality of their small lives. Besides, this little worker, Thora, had a such a talent for dreaming. A wild white rose, in the midday sun. And nectar. What a wonderful piece of visualization. It was more than a dream, it was a sensual experience, practically. Especially that bit about nectar.

Alfred tried hard not to think too much about that part of Thora's dream. It was unfortunate that she had dreamed about nectar. It made him think of honey. He really had tried not to. He had taken hardly any honey since yesterday, just a cell full for breakfast and a mid-morning snack. All in all he had done rather well. Surely a little tipple now, so late in the day, would do no harm. He deserved it, after all. When he had convinced himself, he ambled off happily to find an uncapped honey cell or one that was ripe for uncapping.

12

the following afternoon he composed another poem. It was a poem about the
sunrise.

The blushing virgin Queen
Of the pale Dawn

Raises her head
In the pure
Stillness of the air.

It was a pity that other drones didn't understand his poetry. He found it quite irritating. They thought his poem was a love poem. It was useless to try to tell them that he had used the unsullied innocence of their virgin Queen merely as a metaphor. What he had meant to express was the pristine quality of the sunrise. Drones came to him, one after another, touched antennae politely with him and made remarks like, "Well done, Alfred, didn't know you had it in you."

Some of the cruder types were more direct. They asked him to recite it again and again and kept interrupting and groaning "Kwagh."

Mo couldn't see why he was so vexed. "It's a pretty good love poem, even if it is about the sunrise," he insisted. "They would understand if they had seen a sunrise."

That morning Belle had come in the darkness before dawn to call them. "Get up, get up," she said shaking Mo first and then Alfred. "You have to inspect the sunrise."

Mo was bewildered. What on earth was a worker doing, wakening him in the middle of the night? For a moment he thought he must still be dreaming.

"Get up," Belle persisted.

"I think it's raining," he said and turned back to sleep.

"No, it's not," she said, giving him another, more vigorous shake.

"All right, all right," he said at last. Alfred was still asleep. How disgusting of him to be asleep when other drones had to get up. "Get up," Mo said, giving Alfred a kick.

"Ouch!" Alfred gasped, starting awake.

Thora came too. As they approached the entrance of the hive they felt the chill air of the early morning and hesitated.

"It's too cold," Mo said, turning to go back.

"You must do it," Belle insisted and pushed him outside.

They huddled together in the gray light, keeping close to the entrance. "Well," Alfred said irritably, "I don't see any sign of the sun. What are you going to do about it?"

Mo hesitated before replying. Was there really anything he could do? Would the sun pay any attention to him? "I suppose it's a bit ridiculous, when you think of it," he said dubiously. "Why should the sun obey a decree of the Grand Council?"

"What?" Alfred asked in a shocked voice.

"Well, do you really think the sun will rise, just because the Council said it must?"

Alfred knew it was merely another of those subversive ideas that Mo liked to come up with. However it wasn't proper to talk like that in front of workers. Workers didn't go in much for thinking. They might have trouble coping with ideas like that. "I'm quite sure the sun will obey the Council's decree," he said to reassure Belle and Thora and then, because he was shivering, he huddled close, squeezing between them for warmth.

They waited a long time. Still no sun appeared.

"There, what did I tell you," Mo said in

exasperation, "the Council can't legislate for the sky."

"Of course it can," Alfred insisted.

"Move over," Belle said suddenly, giving Alfred a push. "I can't see."

"See what?" Alfred turned to look where she was looking and caught his breath. In the east, behind the hill, where the sky had been glowing with light for some time, the sun raised a pale rim above the skyline. Silently the bees watched. It rose, bit by bit, into the sky and spread its light sideways along the threshold of the hive. They stood silent for a long time, just looking.

"Isn't it wonderful," Belle whispered, but Thora hushed her. Words were inadequate for the glory of light and sun and pearly cloud that spread slowly across the eastern sky.

"Why?" Mo whispered to himself softly, and realized that his question was trivial and futile. At such a moment it was enough to be, without having to know why.

When the full shining circumference had risen above the horizon, he sighed with deep satisfaction. "I'll report to the Grand Council that the sun is observing its decree," he said, conscious, for the first time, of the ineffable importance of his position as Inspector of Sunlight.

"And I'll write a poem," Alfred added with quiet emotion.

They were disturbed in their reflections by a stream of field bees leaving the hive, setting out in search of the first supplies of the morning.

"We'd better go back to work," Belle said, turning to go inside. Thora followed.

the following night Thora dreamed
again. This time it was not a pleasant dream.
She would have preferred not to have a dream
at all than to have such a terrible nightmare.
She dreamed of noise and commotion, of

screams of terror, and of a long shaft of golden light that lit a pale amber figure and made it glow.

In the morning she tried to tell Belle about her dream, but Belle answered crossly and went off alone on a cleansing flight.

"Any dreams last night?" Alfred asked when he came to Thora to be groomed and fed.

Thora nodded. "It wasn't a nice dream." She regurgitated some honey and let him sip it from her tongue. Then as she combed and cleaned him, she struggled to describe the unpleasant impression her dream had made.

Alfred was intrigued. This little worker was really imaginative in her small way. "A figure?" he asked interestedly. "Clean that bit in there," he said, raising a wing to let her get at the tender membrane between his segments.

"It was a pale figure, lit by a long, shining light."

"And noise? Do be careful. I have a very sensitive chitin shell."

Thora brushed more gently. "There was a lot of noise."

"Perhaps your dream has a meaning."

"A meaning? Can you spread your wings a little more?"

"Mmm. That's wonderful. I'll ask the Grand Drone for you. He understands dreams."

"I don't think you should go to the Grand Drone," Mo objected, when Alfred told him about it. "You know what he's like. He sees all sorts of meanings in the simplest things."

"It can't do any harm, checking out a dream."

"Don't encourage him."

Mo did not quite believe in the Grand Drone. Apart from the fact that the elder drone had disregarded all democratic procedures when he appointed himself Grand Drone of the hive, he had more recently assumed even greater powers and declared himself sacred intermediary of the Great Drone in the Sky.

Mo thought he could remember that before the departure of the swarm, there had been a democratically elected Grand Council and no Grand Drone at all. However when he mentioned this to Alfred, Alfred could remember nothing about it.

"Are you quite sure you didn't dream it?" he asked.

Mo wasn't sure that he didn't. But still he had doubts. The trouble was, the Grand Drone overdid his new role. He claimed to be the only channel of communication between drones and the GDS. He was the one to whom were revealed the mysteries. Only through him could any drone intercede. Mo was skeptical. He was nearly sure he could remember a time when any drone could invoke the GDS on his own account.

Workers, of course, were not initiated. The revelations of the Great Drone were exclusively for drones. The Divinity did not concern Himself with females. Female worker bees and even the Queen were the earthbound children of an earthly Queen and her earthly consort. Only through the agency of drones could the Queen be raised up to be the great universal mother, progenitrix of the hive.

Drones, on the other hand, had no earthly father. Mo was glad he was born a drone, not one of the small ignorant workers who eked out their humble existence in daily servitude, blind to the greatness of the destiny of drones.

While he was dissatisfied with the pronouncements of the Grand Drone, he had no real grievance. The Grand Drone was generous with his revealed knowledge and was always pleased to initiate other drones into any fresh mysteries. Even Alfred, who was a genius in his way, considered it an honor to be noticed by the Grand Drone and Mo, now that he had been appointed Inspector of Sunlight, wondered if he should not perhaps accept things as they were. If the world needed to be set right, why should he have to do it? It would be so much easier not to.

Alfred was happy to accept things as they were. He had no misgivings about telling Thora's dream to the Grand Drone. The Grand Drone was kindly and harmless. Did it matter if he wanted to be sole intermediary and interpreter of mysteries? As Grand Drone he was deeply interested in the subject of dreams. Even the dream of a worker would be of interest to him.

However Alfred did not have the opportunity

to mention the matter immediately. The Queen appeared earlier than usual on the threshold board and for a while, he was preoccupied.

This time the Queen circled the hive in wider circles than previously. The drones flew up high above and watched appreciatively.

After a brief hesitation, Alfred flew up too. He despised the crude drones who shouted remarks and felt unpleasantly out of place in their company, but he could not bear to risk a repeat of the humiliation and embarrassment of his previous meeting with the Queen. Once in the air, he agitated his wings vigorously for several minutes in an effort to improve his fitness and strength. When he grew breathless, he alighted on an apple leaf to rest. In a while he would exercise some more.

Meanwhile the Queen remained outside for several minutes and flew farther from the hive than before. Any day now she would take her first nuptial flight and Alfred feared that he would not be ready. Unless some unforeseen event occurred.

He toyed endlessly with the idea of an unforeseen event. What if the competition for Queen took other qualities into account, not merely brute strength? Was it not an inane way to choose a royal consort, to choose a drone for his physical prowess? Would the Queen really wed the drone who could fly fastest and highest? Could she really want to mate with some muscle-bound chitin-head who would neither appreciate her nor the honor of being her lover?

Alfred could see no reason why the Queen should not change the rules. She ought to look for other qualities such as intelligence, sensitivity, culture. He could offer her all of these. They would be enduring qualities. Not even Mo could be considered a rival to Alfred if intellectual qualities were taken into account. True, Mo was something of a philosopher, but he lacked poetry. He did not share Alfred's sensibility, his idealistic adoration of the virgin soul of the Queen and her unsullied innocence. These were what attracted Alfred, not her mere physical loveliness.

When the Queen went inside he forced himself to fly all the way to the nearest drone-congregating spot just for exercise. The effort made him breathless and he had to rest when he reached the spot. It was an elevated place, above a grassy knoll, several fields away on the other side of the river. There he listened to the bragging talk of drones from his own and other hives. *They should hear themselves,* he thought irritably. *They all tell the same lies and boast the same stupid boasts.*

Now a skinny young drone was holding forth, telling how he had done without honey for a whole morning because the Great Drone had commanded him to fast from honey till he had won his virgin Queen.

"No honey?" Daisy whined, making a sound like a gnat, "no honey for the drones? What will the drones do without honey?"

The Grand Drone felt obliged to intervene. Communications from the GDS were exclusively his concern. "You've been talking with the Great Drone?" He questioned the young drone with quiet scorn. "When did this happen?"

He always made a point of snubbing pushy

young drones of this sort. This one wasn't old enough even to have been properly initiated into the Cult of the Great Drone, and here he was claiming to be receiving messages from Him, as if he were Grand Drone himself.

"Well?"

"It was in my dream last night," the young drone said.

"Don't be ridiculous. You don't know what you're talking about."

"I did dream it. I heard the voice of the GDS speaking to me in my dream."

"And this voice told you to abstain from honey?"

"Yes."

"No honey for the drones," Daisy wailed. "No honey."

"Be quiet," Guy said fiercely, and Daisy stopped wailing though he continued to buzz intermittently in a distressed tone.

The Grand Drone spoke indignantly. "Don't you know that the Great Drone is the Giver of Honey, that in eating honey we serve Him?"

"I hadn't thought of that," the young drone said uneasily.

"Your dream is an evil dream and tells you to do evil," the Grand Drone went on in a formidable voice.

The young drone quailed. "I'm sorry, I'm very sorry," he said.

"Sorry?"

Alfred felt sympathy for the young drone. With a sense of guilt he remembered his own failed attempt to eat less honey. He hadn't considered the issue in moral terms. His only thought had been to try to make himself more attractive to the young Queen. Of course the Grand Drone was right, drones had a moral duty to consume honey.

"Yes, I'm sorry," the young drone murmured abjectly.

The Grand Drone was satisfied. He spoke more kindly. "Go home to your hive, young drone, and have some honey. Lots of honey. And do not listen to evil spirits that speak to you in your dreams."

The young drone retired gratefully from the grassy knoll and flew back to the hive.

The Grand Drone turned to the elders. "Young drones, they're all the same. Dreamers of foolish dreams," he said wisely.

Alfred remembered Thora's dream. He approached the Grand Drone and spoke in a respectful voice. "Speaking of dreams," he said, "one of the female workers had a very odd dream last night."

"A worker had a dream?" the Grand Drone asked with interest. "They don't usually dream, do they?"

"No, apparently they don't. But we've been educating this little one, trying to improve her lot."

"Improve her lot?" the Grand Drone asked severely. "Has she been complaining?"

"No, of course not," Alfred explained. "It's just that Mo and I have been telling the workers about some of the finer things of life, on wet days you know, when they're not doing much. We don't distract them from their duties."

"I see." The Grand Drone was mollified. Duty loomed large in his scheme of things. Even workers were bound by his concept of duty.

Alfred elaborated. "Well, this little bee had a very odd dream. She heard a lot of noise and saw a pale, shining figure, the color of honey, lit by a shaft of light."

"The color of honey," the Grand Drone echoed. "Amazing. Why should such a revelation be made to a worker? A female?"

Before Alfred could answer, Guy interrupted. He was always hanging about wherever the Grand Drone was. "The GDS must have His reasons," he suggested with a pious nod of his head. "It is not for us to question His ways." In religious matters Guy was extremely orthodox. He managed to keep his earthly yearning for virgin Queens quite separate from his otherworldly devotion to the GDS.

"A figure the color of honey, lit by golden light," the Grand Drone said reverently. "Yes, it must be Him, the Great Drone in the Sky, Giver of honey, Giver of all."

"The Giver of honey, the Giver of all," several

drones echoed, lapsing without thinking into the litany of praise.

"Lit by a shaft of light," the Grand Drone said, pondering aloud. "Certainly it is a good omen. It augurs well. But why has He made His revelation through a worker?"

"Why?" Mo wondered all that afternoon. "Why a worker?"

The answer that came to him was sudden and startling, like a flash of lightning. "Why not?" he asked himself again and again as he brooded on the matter. "Why not?"

thora discovered that she was an
object of interest. Drones pointed her out to
other drones when she appeared on the threshold
for a cleansing flight. Some of them spoke to her
and asked her if she had had any more dreams.

The Grand Drone stopped her once and asked her name.

"Thora," she answered shyly.

Guy prodded her indignantly. "Bow when you speak to the Grand Drone."

Startled to find herself in conversation with such an important dignitary, Thora bowed deeply.

"Are you happy, Thora?" the Grand Drone asked.

"Yes, I think so." She hadn't really thought about the matter but she would, as soon as she had time to.

"You are not discontented with your lot, I hope?"

"No."

The Grand Drone patted her head. "A good little female is always contented with her lot. If you dream again of the Great Drone you must come at once and tell me."

"If I dream?"

"Yes, if you dream again, let me know. You may go now."

Obediently Thora flew away, and when nobody was watching her she flew across to a place
in the meadow where wild briar twined among
the boughs of a hawthorn hedge. The briar was
in bloom. Thora chose a delicately scented blossom that had opened its petals only that morning. It held a single drop of dew. She sipped
some of the dew into her nectar sac and then lay
among the soft velvety petals, trying to feel irresponsible and carefree as she had done in her
dream.

She looked at the sky and at the green leaves
of the overhanging hedge. She tried hard to be
idle, to think idle thoughts, but it was no use.
She kept remembering that Belle was waiting
for her to come back and help her carry honey
down from the upper storage combs to the lower
ones to replace the quantities of honey that the
drones had eaten the day before. In vain she tried
to convince herself that somebody else would
help. She kept feeling the urge to go back to the
hive and do her share. Again and again she tried
to repress the feeling but it wouldn't go away.
She gave up after a few minutes and flew back to

the hive. It seemed she had no real talent for idleness, in spite of her dream.

"What kept you?" Belle asked irritably.

Thora hurried to help. Belle's abdomen was distended with honey and she crawled slowly along the brood comb. She chose a cell that was already half-filled, stopped, and filled it to its brim. Thora helped some younger bees who had been secreting wax to cap and seal the cell, then hurried after Belle to bring more honey from the stores in the upper frames.

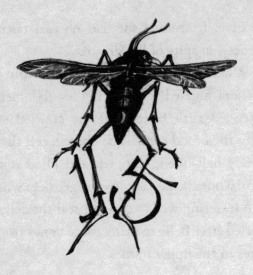

over the days that followed, Mo pondered deeply. It was, he realized, principally a matter of seeing things in a new way. It meant unlearning old attitudes and looking at ideas as if one were formulating them for the first time. When he began to question things that everybody had taken for granted, he found that one question led to another and the old certainties crumbled.

Why, for example, should females devote themselves to nurturing young and producing food? Were they not just as capable of higher feeling and thought as drones were? Why should drones consider themselves superior?

He could think of no good reason for workers to be kept always at the lowest level of existence, slaving endlessly at the meaningless drudgery of the hive while drones enjoyed a higher existence of spirit and mind. Why not raise workers from their lowly status? They could be educated. They could learn to used their minds in the pursuit of literature, philosophy, the sciences. Why should they not fulfill themselves just as fully as drones? Endlessly he debated the question with Alfred. "Is a worker not equal to a drone?" he argued.

"Which worker do you mean, which drone?" Alfred answered sardonically. He was hanging upside down within the spherical umbel of one of the tall angelica flowers that grew among the willows on the riverbank. Mo, more energetic, was sitting upright on one of the small florets that made up the umbel. Alfred didn't really see any point in discussing the enlightenment of workers. Things were the way they were and why bother changing them?

"And other creatures," Mo argued, going on to a fresh subject, "why do we persist in treating them as our enemies?"

"Which other creatures?"

"Well, wasps for example."

"Wasps? You wouldn't consider associating with wasps?" Alfred righted himself and started indignantly to his feet.

"Why not?"

"Because . . . you know why . . . because wasps are low, nasty, brutish creatures."

"You're reacting emotionally. You've been conditioned to hate wasps, but you can't give valid reasons for hating them."

"They're thieves and murderers," Alfred insisted.

"Can you prove that?"

"Everybody says so."

"Exactly, everybody says so. But what everybody says is not necessarily true. It may be that some individual wasps have unpleasant ways but that is no reason to blame all wasps. Like ourselves, wasps are free to choose. A wasp may be just as decent a fellow as a bee."

"Which bee, which wasp?" Alfred replied, sardonic again.

that evening, when the sun was
setting and the bees were gathering into the
hive, a momentous event occurred. The GDS
manifested Himself.

Guy had gone deep inside the hive, as he usually did at the end of the day, to ask a worker bee

to feed and groom him. He was regular in his habits and preferred to have his meals at set intervals rather than taking potluck with passing workers on the threshold, as a lot of less fitness-conscious drones did.

He was in a passageway near the brood chamber when it happened. A thin beam of light appeared miraculously in the darkness of the hive. He watched it grow longer and wider and then, before his eyes, the GDS revealed Himself. The apparition was just as the little worker bee had seen it in her dream. The Great Drone's pale limbs shone golden, glowing in honey-colored light. His eyes were deep shadows. Around and above, the air was filled with the low humming of bees busy about their work, but the GDS made no sound or movement.

Guy was seized with fear and trembling and bowed low. When he dared look up again the GDS had disappeared and there was only darkness where the golden light had been. Overwhelmed with awe, he hurried to tell the Grand Drone what he had seen.

The Grand Drone was just settling down for

the night in the warm center of the brood comb. "Whatever do you mean, 'revealed Himself'?" he asked crossly, when Guy came excitedly to tell his story.

"I saw Him," Guy insisted, "in the corner of the passageway, near the rear of the chamber."

"Have you been having a honey binge?" The Grand Drone looked closely at Guy for signs of intoxication.

"I haven't had any honey, not since this afternoon," Guy insisted. He was speaking the truth. He was abstemious in his habits insofar as any drone could be called abstemious.

"Show me," the Grand Drone said finally.

"But He's not there now. He disappeared."

"You're telling me you saw the GDS, shining with light just as the worker saw Him in her dream, and then He disappeared?"

"Yes."

"What did He say to you?"

"Nothing."

"Nothing?"

The Grand Drone deliberated. There could be no doubt that Guy had seen something out of the ordinary. Drones who had been settling down to sleep a minute previously were wide awake now and crowded around expectantly.

"I will think about your vision, if it is a vision," the Grand Drone said finally, "and tomorrow we will decide what, if anything, is to be done."

As the bees settled down to sleep, the story of the apparition was told over and over. It spread from the warm center of the cluster where the drones slept to the outer edge where the field bees, who preferred the cooler temperature, liked to sleep. Belle and Thora slept with the hive workers, sandwiched between the drones on the inside and the field bees on the outside. When Belle heard the story she was indignant. "Now look what you've done," she scolded Thora, "you and your silly dreams."

"But it's not my fault," Thora protested. "I didn't know it would make them go seeing things."

"You shouldn't encourage their nonsense," Belle insisted.

Other young workers listened with awe. They

realized that the worker bee who had dreamed a prophetic dream was right there in the cluster with them. They pointed out Thora to each other and chattered eagerly about Guy's vision. The next morning two of them claimed they had been dreaming in the night and instead of going to work, they went off to tell the Grand Drone about their dreams.

17

the next day drones came and went excitedly in the passages around the brood chamber. They got in the way of workers and soiled the cells that had been cleaned in readiness for when the young Queen would be ready to lay. It was not till afternoon, when the Queen flew out on her daily orientation flight, that the drones at last left the hive to the workers and followed her outside.

They did not stay long out-of-doors. The Queen came back in a few minutes. Shortly afterward the sky, which had been clear and blue for several days, grew overcast and a rumble of thunder preceded a heavy downpour of rain. Above the hum of bees could be heard the steady sound of raindrops pattering on the roof of the hive.

The drones gathered inside, snug and dry in the middle of the brood chamber, discussing eagerly the event of the previous evening. Guy was the center of a throng and had to tell his story over and over.

The Grand Drone stayed on the other side of the comb, aloof from the throng, meditating profoundly. He took a long time over his deliberations but at last, toward evening, gave his decision in the matter. "We will go to the passageway now, this very evening, and see if the GDS will appear again."

This time there were careful preparations. It

would not be enough to see the GDS reveal Himself. They would do homage properly.

"Count me out," Mo said skeptically and detached himself from the crowd who were already forming themselves into a procession. Alfred, however, hurried to join in.

"You're not really going, are you?" Mo asked.

"Why not?"

"You think the GDS showed Himself to a chitin-head like Guy?"

"Not really. I'm just going along to see the fun. Come on, it'll be good for a laugh."

"Well, if you put it that way," Mo said, suddenly stirred by curiosity, and he pushed his way into the line.

The procession of drones extended in a wide circle, two rings deep, on the floor of the hive. The more devout had already begun to chant the litany of the GDS while they were lining up. Now the procession was ready to begin.

Slowly it wound its way in and out through the passageways of the hive. The two young workers who had come to tell the Grand Drone their dreams were the only workers involved.

The Grand Drone had appointed them vestal virgins and now they carried gifts of pollen and honey for the GDS and reverently walked backward before the Grand Drone as if he were a Queen.

Guy had submitted to follow two paces behind the Grand Drone, although he disputed this arrangement at first. He felt that he, as the chosen one, ought to lead the way. However the Grand Drone was much more skilled at argument, and Guy was quickly persuaded that only a Grand Drone could properly lead the procession. As a concession, he was allowed to have Daisy walk behind in attendance on him.

They moved solemnly along the brood combs, obstructing the workers who were capping cells. "Go away," they exclaimed, "you can't come this way." The drones, absorbed in their devotions, seemed oblivious to the workers and trampled on the fresh cell cappings, breaking several of them.

At last they came to the holy place where the GDS had appeared. The procession halted. Hundreds of the drones crushed into the passageway, pushing and climbing on top of each other for a better view. Guy went to the spot where he had stood the previous evening, and waited.

Above the excited hum of drones they could hear the rain still drumming steadily on the roof, and from far away came the faint growl of thunder. The atmosphere was tense.

Would the GDS reveal Himself again? Would He give a sign? Again and again the Grand Drone led the chanting of the praises of the GDS and the passageway echoed to the voices of the hundreds of drones who gave the responses..

"Giver of nectar . . ."

"Light in the sky . . ."

"Dew on the petal . . ."

"Summer shower . . ."

"Great Giver of all . . ."

"Great Drone in the Sky . . ."

Night fell, but inside the hive there was only darkness. Nothing happened. No miraculous shaft of light appeared. There was no sign.

"What did I tell you, didn't I say the GDS wouldn't reveal himself to Guy?" Mo whispered to Alfred.

"Shush," drones hissed from all sides.

They waited for a long time and then, disappointed, went back to the brood chamber to sleep. The Grand Drone and Guy were the last to leave the passageway. They consoled themselves by eating the honey that the two workers had carried as gifts.

"You may go now," the Grand Drone said loftily when they offered him pollen as well.

"What will we do with the pollen?" they asked.

"Oh put it back wherever you got it," he said irritably. "Leave it there till next time."

The two workers bowed deeply and went away.

18

in the morning a mist lay white as clover honey over the orchard. Workers who went out on cleansing flights saw the ghostly shapes of apple trees and heard the river, swollen by the previous night's rain, make a rushing sound which carried across the meadow on the still air. In the hive there was an air of expectancy. Although the workers did their usual chores as carefully as always, their minds were not on their work. They felt a vague sense that today would not be a day like other days.

The bees who were closest to the Queen that morning fussed over her, offering food, brushing and stroking her, and making her ready for the day ahead. The Queen herself was restless and paced over and back incessantly, obliging her attendants to move over and back along with her.

"Please, your majesty, do stand still," an attendant asked her politely when she had to start all over again to brush the fine hair of her head.

"How can I stand still?" the Queen asked in an agitated voice. "How can I stand still on this day of all days?" Again and again she approached the hive entrance and then drew back.

By mid-morning the mist had given way to hazy sunshine. The hive entrance was bathed in light, and the drones who had slept late after the previous night's ceremonies went outside to hover in the sunlight above the threshold. Shortly after noon they grew noisy and excited.

They caught the expectant mood of the hive and wondered what was afoot.

The Grand Drone, still waiting for a sign, any sign, wondered if today might not be the day. "We must wait," he said gravely, "we must wait till we are given a sign."

"A sign of what?" Mo demanded.

"A sign of our great destiny," the Grand Drone answered and then, realizing the question was irreverent, turned, frowning, to see who had spoken.

"What destiny?" Mo persisted.

The Grand Drone disdained to reply.

"You shouldn't talk like that to the Grand Drone," Alfred said when the Grand Drone had moved to the other side of the threshold.

"He shouldn't talk such piffle," Mo retorted. "He can't expect us to believe in Guy's drunken hallucinations."

"The Grand Drone says he wasn't drunk."

"He must have been." Mo had tried to trust the Grand Drone but found it impossible. He was so full of bombast, always talking about signs and destiny. Destiny indeed. What was destiny? A high-sounding word that didn't mean a lot. The Grand Drone could fool all the drones some of the time, and some of the drones all the time, but . . . but what? Mo pondered deeply. There was a profoundly subversive thought in there somewhere, if he could just find words for it.

For the moment, most drones wanted to believe. Guy was the center of a large concourse who, in spite of the non-appearance of the GDS the previous evening, still wanted to hear again and again the story of his vision. Occasionally a devotee, overcome by the miraculous account, would break into praise.

"Giver of honey . . . Light of the sun . . . Summer shower . . . Father of all."

"Great Father of all," hundreds of drones chanted in response.

Overwhelmed by the fervor of the moment, the Grand Drone announced that on such a sacred occasion the drones should not indulge in their usual afternoon Queen quest. "Let us stay here all afternoon and sing His praises," he proposed.

"No way," Guy objected indignantly, "the GDS didn't say anything about not going Queen-questing."

"The GDS said nothing at all to you," the Grand Drone reproached him.

Guy disregarded the Grand Drone's protests and flew up into the air. A huge throng of drones followed. They hovered above the orchard humming loudly. In a few minutes swarms of drones arrived from other hives. The hovering cloud of drones grew massive and black. Excitement rose.

For a while Alfred remained on the threshold. He fully intended to fly up and join the other drones, but would not do so just because Guy had defied the Grand Drone. He would go in his own good time.

Mo paced on the threshold, ignoring what was happening overhead. He was thinking deeply on his newest profound thought. You can fool all of the drones all of the time, and some of the drones some of the time. No that wasn't what he was trying to say. It was difficult to concentrate. The business of the Queen was an intolerable distraction even though he was doing his utmost not to notice the commotion in the air.

"Aren't you going Queen-questing today?" Alfred asked.

"Not today, I've a profound thought to work out."

"Oh." Alfred hesitated an instant, then flew away to join the crowd of drones.

Only Mo and the Grand Drone were left on the threshold. "How can they seek their destiny when they go Queen-questing every day?" the Grand Drone asked, looking up in vexation at the black cloud that began to buzz in a frenzy of excitement. The virgin Queen had appeared at the entrance of the hive.

Languidly she stretched herself. Her slender body glistened in the sunlight. Slowly she spread her wings and flew out and up, making a wide, graceful circle in the air.

It was more than the Grand Drone could stand. He forgot his solemn resolution and flew up. Mo tried hard to concentrate. "You can drone some of the time all the fools," he mumbled distractedly and then paused abruptly. Sometimes profound thoughts were not enough. There were some things that were more important. He spread his wings and flew up, humming loudly.

The cloud of drones hovered expectantly as the Queen circled the hive, and then the moment they had been waiting for came. She flew upward, passed swiftly among them, and dashed away. Frenziedly they followed.

She flew higher and higher. She passed over a tall hawthorn hedge, crossed a meadow where grass grew lush and deep, then flew up a green hillside. Alfred, to his surprise, found himself among the leaders in the pursuit. Spurred by passion perhaps. He had not supposed he could.

Guy was just ahead, followed closely by a dozen or so other drones. The Queen passed over the hilltop and down into the hollow beyond. The drones followed, skimming the top branches of a grove of poplars. Still the Queen soared upward and onward. Just when Alfred was gasping for breath and thought he must fall back out of the chase, the Queen paused in mid-flight and turned to face her pursuers.

Guy was there first. He closed with the Queen in a brief embrace. Alfred drew up short and hovered close to them, quivering with jealous rage. He heard the faint click of Guy's progenitive organs popping from inside to out. He witnessed Guy's instant of bliss and saw him drop, still locked in deadly embrace, to the ground.

If only he had been a little faster, he could have been the one. Alfred was overwhelmed with deep disappointment. What greater bliss could there be than to be the beloved, the sole lover of the Queen? Already a poem began to take shape in his mind. His disappointment in love would be the great tragedy of his life, the great theme of his poetry.

The Queen suddenly flew up, abandoning Guy on the ground. She looked round at the drones who had followed her all the way and caught sight of Alfred.

"Who's next?" she asked with a silly giggle.

Alfred drew back, deeply shocked. Surely his

Queen did not mean to mate with another drone?

The Queen did mean to. She chose another drone and then another. Some of them clicked. Some of them popped. All of them died.

She chose drones who did not even belong to her own hive, drones that had come Queen-questing from other hives. Alfred watched in horrified fascination. His barely conceived poem withered and died. The great theme of his life became a horrible farce. He had idealized this Queen. He had attributed to her all the virtues of queenhood: purity, faithfulness, honor. A Queen who would preserve her own honor and the honor of her hive. Now he watched her degrade herself. One after another she received her lovers and then wrenched herself free of them. Dead and dying lovers littered the ground.

At last she was sated. She did not even glance at Alfred who still hovered, sick at heart. He almost wished he had been one of the dead, faithless though she was. Would it not have been better to die in bliss and ignorance than live in disenchantment forever? He paused in his gloomy meditation. Perhaps there was something to be salvaged.

Disenchantment could be a theme for poetry. A drone who has seen the falsity, the futility of love would have much to say to the world. He settled himself comfortably on a purple-headed thistle to consider the matter.

the workers who had waited anxiously outside the hive for the return of the Queen were relieved when at last she alighted on the threshold.

"Well?" they asked.

The Queen nodded and turned to show them, trailing behind her the trophies of her matings. The torn organs of drones were proof of her fecundation. The workers were satisfied and joyfully escorted her into the hive. Now the future was assured.

The drones returned singly or in small groups in the course of the afternoon. They came quietly, without the elation that had marked their setting forth. Nobody spoke of the Queen nor of the drones who didn't come back, and when the Grand Drone remembered that it was time to go and pay homage to the GDS they roused themselves and lined up eagerly, glad of an excuse to think of something else.

Alfred and Mo fell into line with the others. Alfred was too absorbed to speak. A bitter, cynical poem was already taking shape in his mind and gave much relief to his wounded soul.

Devoutly they followed the Grand Drone as he led the procession into the passage beside the brood chamber. Nobody mentioned Guy or that the vision was his. Guy's name was one of those unspeakable things that were best forgotten. The Grand Drone was once again sole intermediary between drones and the GDS. Their destiny, was, after all, something higher and nobler than Queen-questing. They would go to the holy place and wait for a sign.

Deep in the honey-scented darkness of the hive they crowded together. A few devout drones began to chant praises but others hushed them. Then the ineffable happened. A shaft of light appeared in the darkness. Slowly it widened. Against the wall, the GDS manifested Himself. He glowed in amber light, wordless, unmoving, gazing with sad, hollow eyes on His sons.

The Grand Drone, overwhelmed, bowed deeply and the rest of the drones did the same. A wild, eerie wail arose. Daisy had cried out in terror. When the drones raised their heads, the GDS had disappeared. Daisy was thrashing frantically on the ground, still crying out. Evidently the vision of the GDS was too overwhelming for a bee who was not all drone. Consoled, the drones fed on honey and retired to the brood chamber to sleep.

"I still think it's a lot of nonsense," Mo said to Alfred as they settled down for the night, but with less conviction than before.

the queen flew out to mate for three days in succession. Neither Alfred nor Mo ever caught up with her. They were among the mass of drones who came back weary, dejected, and disappointed. They avoided looking each other in the eye, each ashamed of his desire and even more ashamed of his failure.

After her last nuptial flight the Queen suddenly stopped being frivolous and giggly.

"Ladies," she announced to the workers in a sensible, matronly tone, "today I will lay eggs."

The brood cells were ready, each one shining clean, ready for use.

"This one, Your Majesty," Belle said, pointing out a cell in the middle of the comb.

The Queen examined it carefully. "A worker cell," she noted with satisfaction. She carefully lowered her abdomen into it and deposited her first egg.

The workers crowded to look and exclaimed with delight when they saw the pale silken thread in the bottom of the cell.

"It will be a worker," Belle said with pleasure.

"Yes," the Queen agreed, "we need more workers, lots of workers. Of course we will have some drone eggs, too, just a few."

"Just a few," the workers agreed.

She laid eggs all day and hive workers clustered on the brood combs to incubate them.

When the eggs hatched into larvae after three days they had to be fed and tended and the burden of work for the hive bees increased considerably. At the same time bees were needed for field work. The main honey flow was under way and the harvest had to be won. Already the upper storage combs were filling up. The work of fanning went on incessantly, to evaporate the honey. When it was ripe it had to be capped with wax. The brood chamber also required extra work and had to be extended again and again to provide for the laying of the fertile young Queen.

Ants became a nuisance, trying to sneak into the hive to steal the ripe, richly scented honey. Bees had to be taken from housekeeping duties to provide extra guards at the hive entrance. By fanning all together, they could create a draft that swept foraging ants right off the threshold board. Thora was sent to guard the entrance, while Belle remained inside, capping honey cells.

Thora was pleased to be outside where she could enjoy the brightness of the sun and its warmth on her wings. Her association with drones had taught her to appreciate such things. However, she worked dutifully with the other workers, in spite of her acquired taste for thinking and dreaming.

"Don't do that," Mo said when he noticed that the workers were blowing ants right off the threshold board. "How can you be so mean to those poor little ants?"

"We have to keep them out of the hive or they would steal honey," Thora explained.

"What makes you think they want to steal honey? Perhaps they've just come visiting."

Thora hesitated. She hadn't ever thought about it. She assumed that ants were enemies because everyone else said so. Now that she thought about it, it seemed hardly reasonable to suppose that such tiny little creatures were a threat to bees.

"Insects should cooperate," Mo argued persuasively. Several interested drones gathered around to listen to him. The fanners continued fanning, but listened curiously to his startling point of view. "We are insects, ants are insects. It is wrong of us to suppose that ants who come to the hive are invariably coming to steal. Has anybody ever asked them why they come?"

The fanning bees looked questioningly from one to the other.

"Who told you to fan ants away?"

"I don't know," Thora said. She turned to the other workers. "Do any of you know?"

They shook their heads.

"We were fanning the air out and then we found that we could fan the ants away, too, that's all," a worker explained.

"So you've been jumping to conclusions," Mo said sternly, "bullying these little creatures, knocking them about. Have you considered that some of them may be injured by falling off the threshold?"

"Look out," a worker called, and turned to fan vigorously as a persistent ant who had already been blown back several times advanced across the threshold once more. Instinctively, Thora and the other workers resumed fanning. The ant rolled over and over, blown backward toward the edge.

"Stop!" Mo shouted. "Stop. Think of what you're doing. You'll hurt it." The workers stopped fanning and Mo helped the tiny ant to roll off its back and stand upright again.

"Are you all right?" he asked courteously.

"Leave me alone," the ant said defensively.

"We're not going to hurt you. We just want to know why you have come to the hive."

"I came to rob honey, what do you think?" the ant said crossly, and turning, squirted a jet of liquid from its tail. Its aim was deadly accurate. The jet struck Mo in his middle simple eye. It burned horribly.

"Ouch!" he cried out, making a futile effort to wipe it away. "Help, help me!" He ran frantically up and down the threshold. Thora and another worker seized him and held him down. They quickly cleaned the formic acid from his eye. Meanwhile, the other workers resumed fanning and vigorously swept the ant off the threshold board.

"Is that better?" Thora asked, licking delicately around Mo's eye with her long tongue.

Mo moaned. It still stung painfully.

"Well," Alfred asked sardonically, "what do you think now of being friendly with ants?"

Mo did not reply.

21

when belle was twenty days old, she
became a field worker. Thora saw her only now
and again in the daytime as she passed by, coming home with full pollen baskets and a bulging
nectar sac, or going out with them empty. They
had time only at night to talk properly to each

other, and then Belle was usually too tired to say much.

"It must be nice to work among flowers all day," Thora said enviously when they were settling down together on the brood comb.

"I never have time to think about it," Belle said with an enormous yawn. "I just collect the nectar and pollen and carry it home."

"Don't you ever just stop to enjoy the flowers and the fresh air?"

"Of course not. I don't have time for anything like that."

Belle was so certain of everything. She could only see one good in existence, the good of the hive. Sometimes Thora wished she could be so single-minded. But to do that, she would have to give up enjoying things personally.

The brood comb filled up rapidly as the Queen laid over a thousand eggs a day. "Aren't you going to lay any drone eggs?" Mo asked the Queen when he noticed she had filled the new brood comb with worker eggs only.

"We have enough drones in this hive already," the Queen answered shortly.

"Don't you want sons?"

"Yes, of course, I did lay a few drone eggs at first. But it's no longer the right time of year for rearing drones. We don't need any more drones till next year."

That was a startlingly new idea to Mo. If drones were masters of the hive and its destiny was theirs, how was it the Queen could make such a decision? Was it possible that she alone, without consultation, could decide whether or not drone eggs were to be laid? He went again and looked at the empty drone cells on the outer edge of the brood. Some of them were being used to store pollen. A few even had honey in them. He paced the threshold for a long time that afternoon, thinking a profounder and more subversive thought than he had ever thought before.

Alfred kept interrupting his thinking. Now that Alfred had become bitter and cynical he was not such pleasant company. He had composed only one poem since the Queen's first nuptial flight. It was a bitter poem, a poem of disenchantment.

When a worker sips rainwater
From a cowpat
May a Queen
Not sip it too?

The poem was an instant success. All the drones were perfectly happy to drink water carried from cowpats or from the stagnant pond near the cow byre. Workers carried it to the hive whenever it was available. It was sweet-tasting, with a faint scent of manure. In fact most of the drones preferred it to dew, which was pure but insipid. However the idea of the plump, matronly Queen with her distended, egg-filled abdomen daintily sipping cowpat water was slightly ludicrous. The drones repeated Mo's new poem appreciatively and soon the word cowpat uttered anywhere in front of the threshold was enough to make them all rock with laughter.

Mo did not join in their amusement. He had profounder thoughts to occupy his mind. Nevertheless he found it difficult to while away the idle hours. Life seemed aimless now that the

Queen had mated. What had become of the great destiny of drones? No one even knew what it would be, although the Grand Drone kept promising a sign.

The evening processions of homage to the Great Drone continued. Some days the GDS did not manifest Himself, but more often He did. The processions were becoming repetitive. The only entertaining bit was when Daisy cried out in terror and threw a fit on the ground each time the GDS was revealed. And even that was the same every time. Mo felt a vague sense of the tedium of existence. There should be more to life than drab daily routine. Even the rising and setting of the sun was repetitive, an endless, meaningless succession of color-daubed skies. Not even profound thought could excite him now. Subversive, radical thinking had begun to pall.

Outside, the air was sultry, the heat clammy. He could fly with Alfred, down the meadow and into the cool shade of the willows on the riverbank, or he could stay where he was and argue about something. Flying to the river would be arduous on such a hot day. He decided to argue.

He would argue with Alfred about the honey dance.

Mo was intrigued by the honey dance. Was it not proof of the creative imagination of workers? Was it not art?

"It cannot be art," Alfred protested. "The honey dance is functional. Art should be . . . er . . ."

"Useless?"

"Well if you want to put it that way. It should be an ornament, it should not have a practical purpose."

"Besides, the movements of the honey dance are so precise, so geometric," a mathematical drone interrupted, taking Alfred's side in the argument. "It is related to mathematics, not art."

Mo clung determinedly to his point of view. It mattered to him. He still meant to be the champion of the workers who had nobody else to speak for them. "The honey dance is artistic expression by workers, females, that's why you refuse to accord it the status of art."

"It's nothing but a message," Alfred countered.

"Isn't a poem a message?"

"Not with a practical purpose."

"In any case, is performance really art?" another drone asked.

"Isn't a poem a performance? It is recited."

"Yes, but a poem is a separate thing," Alfred argued. "Can you tell the dance from the dancer?" Mo had no answer to that, so Alfred won the argument for the time being.

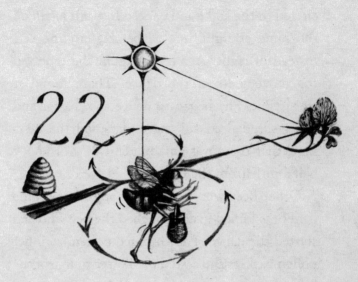

thora was working on a honeycomb
when she first saw the honey dance. A field bee
came in, carrying nectar, which she offered to
the other bees to taste. Then she began to dance.
She danced in a straight line on the honeycomb, wagging the tail end of her rump, then

circled to the right and danced forward again on the same straight line as before, circling left instead of right. Again and again she repeated the movements of the dance. Thora found it irresistible. She began to dance too. Faster and faster she danced till she understood the message, that there was an abundant flow of honey half a mile from the hive.

Other bees who were old enough to become field bees joined in and touched the bee who had started the dance. They nibbled pollen from her pollen baskets and tasted the flower source of the honey. When the field bee turned and flew out of the hive, they followed her. Thora paused on the threshold to get her bearings. The dance had told the precise angle between the sun, the hive, and the honey, so she knew which way to go. Quickly she flew away and in less than a minute found herself in a field of soft after-grass where a late crop of white clover had unexpectedly bloomed. She flew down excitedly and alighted on a flower. She reached her long tongue deep into one of its many florets and drew the sweet scented nectar into her honey sac. Busily she hummed, flying from flower to flower till it was time to carry her harvest back to the hive.

She worked all day and when the sun set she was almost too tired to talk to Belle as they settled down together on the brood comb to sleep.

"Well, what kind of day did you have?" Belle asked.

"I was out in a clover meadow," Thora replied.

"And did you enjoy the sunlight and the fresh air and the flowers?"

Thora realized, with astonishment, that she had forgotten to enjoy them. She had been far too busy.

23

if it were not for Mo's attempts to improve the world, things might have continued like that. Thora and Belle flew out each day shortly after sunrise and worked till sunset. They gathered nectar into their honey sacs, and when they came back to the hive they regurgitated it to young house bees who waited inside the hive entrance to relieve field bees of their burden.

When pollen was needed they rolled about in the flowers covering their hairy bodies with pollen. Then they combed it off and packed it carefully into the pollen baskets on their back legs. Even on other errands they carried a little pollen away, because it got caught up on their body hair when they were harvesting nectar.

The hive needed water too. When it was very hot a lot of water was needed to evaporate inside the hive and keep it cool.

They met Alfred and Mo only rarely. Sometimes, as they alighted on the threshold, one or another drone held out his tongue to them, asking to be fed, or nodded his head and stamped his feet in a grooming invitation. It wasn't really Thora and Belle's work anymore. Young hive bees were supposed to take care of the drones, but if the drone who asked was Mo or Alfred, Thora and Belle always obliged. When it rained and they spent the day indoors they had more time to talk and share news of what each had been doing.

Mo was anxious to ask a lot of questions about the role of the Queen and the workers as decision makers in the hive, but Belle and Thora were puzzled when he asked about things that were so obvious.

"Who decides whether to lay drone eggs or worker eggs?" Mo asked persistently.

To Belle it seemed a silly question. "The Queen lays drone eggs in drone cells and worker eggs in worker cells."

"But who decides?"

"Nobody decides. We just know."

"The hive doesn't need any more drones now," Thora tried to explain.

"But who decides that?"

"Nobody decides. It's obvious," Belle replied. "What use are drones? They do no work. They mess up the hive. They gorge on honey and have to be fed and tended like larvae."

"Well, they are useful at night for keeping the brood warm," Thora said. She felt that Belle was going a bit far. Mo and Alfred might take offense.

"That's not useful," Belle retorted. "They just like the warmest place and we let them have it."

Alfred was not offended. "Really," he said with amused tolerance, "what amazing notions you little workers come up with. You know perfectly well that you let us have the warmest place because the best place is reserved for the masters of the hive."

"Hmph," Belle said, and turned her tail end to him.

Mo didn't ask any more questions. He was thinking deeply.

the very next afternoon Mo raised the question of female emancipation before the Grand Council. "There is an injustice in the hive," he began. "The workers toil all day every day while we laze about here in front of the threshold pretending that we are masters of the hive."

His remarks caused an uproar.

"What do you mean, laze about?" the Grand Drone asked indignantly. "We devote ourselves tirelessly to the government and proper regulation of the hive."

"No, we don't," Mo explained. "We pretend to. Do you know that there are no drone eggs being laid in the hive? Who made that decision? Not the drones. None of you knows anything about it, do you?"

This caused a commotion. Angry drones shouted that they would rather die than allow such a decision to be made. Mo had to raise his voice to be heard.

"Nobody is asking you to make that decision. It has already been made by the females, the Queen and the workers."

"Then we will reverse that decision," the Grand Drone said decisively.

"How will you do that?" Mo asked. "The workers are many and we are few. We depend on them totally. They feed us, clean us, give us the warmest part of the brood chamber to sleep in."

"And why shouldn't they," said the Grand Drone, "it is their duty, indeed their privilege, to serve us."

"Why should it be so?" Mo asked. "I propose that drones do their fair share of the work of the hive. . . ." His words were drowned by shouts of outrage from the drones. He paused till the noise subsided. "And I propose that workers be allowed to sit on the Grand Council."

He had gone too far. He had exceeded the boundary line between the outrageous and the ridiculous. Drones rolled about helplessly in midair and shook with laughter. Even the Grand Drone allowed himself to snigger. "Let's have cowpats on the Grand Council," someone called out, and the drones roared with delight.

Mo, crestfallen, turned to Alfred. "Didn't any of what I said make sense to you?"

"No."

The Grand Drone called the meeting to order. "Well, Mo," he said benignly, "have you any more proposals to make?" A few rowdy drones stamped their feet on the roof of the hive to show their amusement and delight and had to be called to order again and again.

"Well, actually I do," Mo said with a defiant air and began to speak again in spite of the noise. "I think we should begin peace negotiations with wasps. They are our nearest relatives in the insect world. We have a great deal in common. We assume, at least the workers assume, that wasps only come to the hive to attack it and so they are driven off. I think we should offer them friendship and cooperation."

There were suppressed titters during this speech. When Mo concluded there was more shouting and stamping of feet. The drones hadn't been so well entertained in a long time. A senior drone rose and shook with mirth as he proposed that Mo should be promoted. Since he had regulated sunlight hours so satisfactorily, the Grand Council should now appoint him ambassador to negotiate peace agreements with creatures outside the hive.

This proposal was received with laughter and cheering.

"What about negotiations with ants?" Alfred shouted and snorted amusedly at his own joke.

Mo hovered with philosophical calm till the laughter subsided. Then, with quiet dignity, he turned to the Great Drone and said, "I accept the position of Ambassador to Creatures Outside the Hive."

"*but wasps* only hang around, hoping to get inside," Belle exclaimed when she heard about Mo's new appointment.

"There you go, stereotyping," Mo argued.

"Wasps are bad," Belle insisted. "Don't try to

tell me that you can make friends with wasps. If you have any sense you'll keep away from them."

Thora remembered his attempt to be nice to an ant, but felt it would be impolite to mention it just now.

The following morning Mo opened negotiations. "Hey, you up there," he called out to a wasp that was weaving from side to side in front of the hive, "may I have a word with you?"

The wasp paused in her flight. "What about?"

"I'm interested in negotiating a peace agreement between bees and wasps," he called out. "I want to talk to you."

The wasp turned and flew away, but returned a few minutes later accompanied by three other wasps. "You down there," she called to Mo who had gone to sleep in the sun.

Mo looked up. "Oh good, you've come back and you've brought your friends, I see. Do come down and have a chat. We have important things to discuss."

The wasps hovered suspiciously.

"It's all right," Mo reassured them, "the Grand Council of Drones has given its approval for communication with wasps."

Cautiously they approached the threshold. Mo flew up eagerly to greet them. Then, without warning, a loud, angry sound arose and a dozen workers who had been guarding the entrance flew fiercely at the approaching wasps.

"No, no, stop!" Mo cried out, but in vain. The workers attacked the wasps, fearlessly showing their stings, which they could use safely against wasps because the barb did not stick in the hard chitin body shell of wasps as it did in the elastic skin of a mammal. The wasps, outnumbered, turned and fled.

The victorious worker bees came back, still quivering with indignation and rage.

"What have you done?" Mo wailed. "Why did you interfere?"

"They were wasps," they said, "we had to chase them away."

"No, you're not supposed to."

"We always chase wasps away."

"Well, you mustn't, not anymore."

"Why not?"

"Because the Grand Council says you're not to."

belle and thora foraged together most of the time. It was harder work now that the main honey flow was over. They had to spend more time looking for flowers. Belle worked faster than Thora at first and made more trips back to the hive, but Thora was more observant and quicker to find flowers that still had a flow of nectar. It was she who found a bank of willow herb in bloom on a warm but dull afternoon when Belle had left her to go back to the hive. Excitedly, she filled her honey sac with nectar and flew home. Mo and Alfred saw her on the threshold and noticed her excitement. "Can we have some nectar?" they asked, extending their tongues, but Thora had no time to stop.

"Sorry, I can't feed you now, ask someone else," she said breathlessly and hurried inside. Mo and Alfred followed, curious to know what was so important. Thora went straight to a honeycomb and offered willow herb nectar to nearby bees. Then she began to dance. It was her turn to lead the honey dance. Ecstatically she moved forward and back on the front of the comb, wagging her rump end faster and faster to show how far away the willow herb was, touching other bees and being touched by them as they joined in the dance.

"She dances very nicely, doesn't she," Alfred commented.

"Absolutely," Mo agreed.

The two drones stamped and moved about a little, wishing they could join in the complicated movements of the dance. With a little practice they could probably learn it.

"Bravo, bravo," Mo called out as one after another, worker bees joined in, eagerly interpreting the story of the dance. It told of honey, at a thirty-degree angle to the sun, just over two miles away. Belle repeated her dance several times, then flew out of the hive followed by workers who already knew, from the dance, the scent and taste of the nectar they were going to seek, in what direction it lay, and how far away.

"That was superb, absolutely superb," Mo said to Thora as she hurried past him, out of the hive. The other workers ended the dance and followed her.

Alfred watched them go. "But it's still not art," he said. Another argument began.

when the Grand Council sat in session again on the subject of female bees, there were several grievances raised and drones, one after another, rose and spoke their vexation and indignation at the generally irresponsible behavior of workers, and their stupidity.

Several drones alluded with anxiety to the point previously raised, that the Queen had not bothered to lay any drone eggs in the new brood comb. This time they had gone and looked for themselves, and confirmed what Mo had observed. Were drones not the key to the future of the hive, its government, religion, and culture? Without drones the hive would be mindless, vegetable almost. What was to be done?

Then the chairdrone of the committee appointed to examine improved methods of cell building reported that workers refused point-blank to implement its recommendations. "I regret to inform the Grand Council that the obsolete hexagonal cell is still in use throughout the hive," he said gravely.

Mo rose to speak. "I have been a champion of workers and their rights," he began, and this time nobody laughed. "However, I must admit that in the matter of my delicate preliminary peace negotiations with wasps, my work has been obstructed by certain worker guard bees at the hive entrance. However I do feel that the solution lies in educating rather than coercing workers. . . ."

He was interrupted by an indignant drone who proposed that females who ignored the edicts and policies of the Grand Council should be punished with the utmost severity of the law. This proposal was applauded and carried almost unanimously. Only Mo and Daisy voted against it.

Daisy, who had never before raised his voice in the assembly, waved for attention as the votes were being counted. "But you can't. How can you?" he chirped loudly.

The Grand Drone turned toward him. "Do you wish to speak, Daisy?" A few drones tittered at the idea of Daisy being allowed to address the Council.

Daisy came right up to the Grand Drone and asked in a small voice, "Who will make the workers do as they're told?"

The Grand Drone looked round the assembly. "We have many able-bodied drones here. I'm sure there will be no shortage of eager volunteers for the position of law enforcement officers."

There was a long silence. Large, burly drones avoided catching anyone else's eye.

"Isn't anyone going to volunteer? No? What about you?" the Grand Drone asked, turning to Daisy. A few titters relieved the tension.

"Not Daisy. Workers have stings," Daisy replied, "Daisy's no fool."

There was a buzz of laughter from some drones, but most remained silent. Then someone proposed an edict ordering workers to comply voluntarily with the law. This more reasonable proposal was carried unanimously and the meeting ended.

the willow herb grew thickly on a damp, clayey bank. Other hives quickly discovered it, too, and hundreds of bees hummed all day among its tall, fragrant blossom. The next meadow was damp and low-lying. Meadow-sweet bloomed in the corners where the grass had not been mowed. The flowers were dusty with pale pollen. When Thora and Belle finished the willow herb harvest they collected nectar and pollen from the meadowsweet. They worked so hard and so long, gathering and carrying, that they were too tired at night to talk to Mo and Alfred.

In any case Mo was a nuisance these days. He kept trying to stop them on the threshold as they came and went, with news of his latest dealings with wasps.

"For heaven's sake, Mo," Belle said in exasperation as she pushed him out of her way for the third time that morning. "Leave those wasps alone."

He was waiting for her when she came out of the hive. "They have given their word, they have promised to respect the security of the hive."

"And you believe them?" Belle flew up in the air.

"Has anyone ever told you, you have a suspicious nature!" Mo called indignantly after her. Then he spotted Thora arriving.

"You're being terribly silly, Mo," Thora said

when he rushed to stand between her and the hive entrance. Couldn't he see that she was burdened with honey?

"But you must listen. This is immense."

"What is?"

"The wasps are coming this afternoon. The Grand Council is gathering in full session to receive them."

"Mo, I haven't time to hear about wasps." Thora, since she had become a field bee, no longer had problems with silly nonsense like dreams and ambitions. Belle had been right all along. The hive was the only thing that mattered. Anything else was an irrelevance. There were winter stores to be laid in and provision to be made for the new brood that would start emerging from their pupae any day now. Soon there would be lots of newly hatched bees to help with the work, but meanwhile the existing workers must do everything.

Early in the afternoon, as Belle and Thora flew home with their burden of honey, they saw the large convocation of drones hovering in front of the threshold. They could not help seeing them because they blocked the hive entrance and got in the way of the workers who were alighting with their harvest and trying to bring it inside. Again and again they wasted workers' precious time, begging to sample nectar and trying to guess which flower it came from.

In the late afternoon, as the sun climbed down the sky and lit the hills with its slanting rays, Thora and Belle set off once more from the damp field of meadowsweet, laden with nectar and pollen. Their first warning that something was amiss came when they met a cloud of drones flying in panic toward them. They did not wait to ask what was wrong. It was obvious that they were urgently needed at the hive.

The wasps had struck with force. Some had penetrated into the hive and some were still engaged in desperate battle in the air and on the threshold. A vibrating, high-pitched hum sounded on all sides. Thora and Belle, prevented by the weight of their harvest from fighting in the air, flew straight to the hive entrance. They alighted beside a group of bees who were bent on driving an invading horde of wasps off the threshold. Furiously they drove forward with their stings exposed. The wasps, too, brandished their stings, and for a few moments the two sides surged forward and back on the threshold.

Then the bees heard a sound that gave them new courage. Inside the hive the song of battle give way to a song of victory. The wasps who had penetrated the hive had been overcome by the hive bees inside. Now the bees rushed outside to reinforce the defenders on the threshold.

Fiercely the phalanx of bees drove the wasps backward. The wasps resisted, yielding only to drive forward again. The bees stung in rage, probing with their sting feelers the tender places between the body segments of the wasps. The wasps stung back with their deadlier venom. Dead bees and wasps were trampled underfoot.

Thora was in the middle of the crush when she heard a cry raised above the song of battle. "Thora," a voice cried, "Thora, help me!" She looked around. Where was Belle? An instant ago she had been fighting alongside, now there was no sign of her. She flew up and hovered an instant above the threshold. She saw what was wrong. Belle had pushed her way to the front line of the defenders. Now she was among the wasps and three of them were attacking her, attracted by her honey sac full of nectar.

Thora flew down beside her and stung fiercely to the left and right. The attackers withdrew and within a minute the threshold was cleared of wasps. The song of victory rose and bees flew off in pursuit of the retreating wasps, but Thora did not join in. She remained on the threshold, head bowed, grieving over the torn corpse of Belle, the best and bravest friend she would ever have.

An hour later the drones came back, quiet and shaken.

"I'm terribly sorry," Mo said again and again. "I had no idea it would end like this. We did not expect them to dishonor their word."

"Belle said it would come to no good," Alfred remembered.

"Why is Belle dead?" Thora asked with a trembling voice.

"Because Mo is an idiot."

"That's not what I mean," Thora said, too

grieved to notice Alfred's frivolous tone. "What I want to know is why bees die?"

Mo and Alfred looked at each other. What sort of question was that? Workers died all the time. It wasn't the sort of thing anybody made a fuss about.

"We work and work," Thora said passionately, "all our lives we do nothing but work and then we die. What is the point of it?"

"I don't know," Mo said as gently as he could.

Thora raised her head and looked at him in bewilderment. "But what is the use of all your profound thinking, what is the use of Alfred's poetry? What use are those things if they don't tell you why?"

"Poetry tells us about the pain of death, not why," Alfred said a little pompously and made a mental note of his remark, which struck him as being very philosophical. He could use it again some time.

Thora asked no more questions. She lowered her head and clutched her dead friend close to her till the hive bees came to clean up and took Belle's corpse away.

mo resolved to retire from public life. His ill-judged peace negotiations had cost workers their lives. "But who could have foreseen that the wasps would break their word?" he asked over and over.

"Belle did," Alfred replied, irritatingly.

"It's only a rhetorical question," Mo said bitterly, "you're not meant to answer it."

"Then stop asking it."

Alfred composed a poem in memory of Belle. It was the least he could do.

> The petal
> In the breath of a summer breeze
> Falls to the ground.

He stopped Thora as she passed him on the threshold and recited it to her. She was grateful and deeply moved. "Thanks, Alfred," she murmured softly.

"It's metaphorical," he explained.

"I know." She paused a moment. "I appreciate it very much," she said, then hurried inside the hive to discharge the contents of her honey sac.

She worked alone now. She had not found a close friend among the other worker bees. A couple of workers who knew of her friendship had come to speak to her about Belle and they mourned a while together, humming plaintively. Then they left Thora alone. She felt tired and old.

In the hive at night, she huddled on the edge of the cluster, comforted by the crush of other bees around her. Now there were more and more very young bees, hatched from the new Queen's brood, who chattered excitedly and gave older bees little opportunity to speak. The young bees were different. They suffered none of the anxiety that Thora's generation had undergone when they lost their Queen. Their future was assured. When they talked they were self-confident and without fear. They spent a lot of time criticizing the drones.

"Drones are unnecessary," one vociferous young worker declaimed loudly. "It's time we got rid of them."

"But some of my best friends are drones," Thora protested.

The young bees laughed outright. "Dirty, lazy drones are your friends? You can't be serious."

"I don't know why we have drones," the

vociferous young worker scolded. She was terribly indignant and reminded Thora a little of Belle, the first time she met her, cleaning up after the drones had messed up a honeycomb.

"I used to have a friend who talked like you," she said.

"Where is she now?"

Thora shook her head and could not bring herself to explain.

The young worker saw her grief. Gently she stroked Thora's head and touched her antennae. "Don't be sad. Your friend has gone to the Earth-Mother. When you go there you will find her."

"Yes. Perhaps it will be so. . . ." Thora hoped so. Alfred's poem came into her head. "The petal, in the breath of a summer breeze, falls to the ground," she said softly to herself.

"What did you say?"

Thora repeated the poem. "A drone composed it for my friend."

"A petal falls to the ground," the young bee repeated with interest, "a drone said that?"

"Yes."

"I suppose some of them are quite intelligent?"

"Some of them, yes."

"But not very many, I suppose?"

"No, not very many," Thora agreed.

when the convocation of drones assembled again, there were grave matters to be considered. One wise elder spoke at length about the general falling off in the quantity and variety of nectar that was being carried home by workers. "It's simply not good enough," he said, "for workers to say that there aren't enough flowers."

"Hear, hear," the drones applauded.

Alfred spoke next. He did not often address the Council. However on the subject of honey he felt strongly. "I speak as a connoisseur," he said. "I have cultivated a fine palate and I must regretfully state that the current flow of nectar is abysmal, quite abysmal. Unworthy of our hive, which, hitherto, has had such a reputation for fine honey."

"The workers must go farther afield and find more flowers," a senior member of the Grand Council proposed.

"Hear, hear," the drones agreed again. They voted unanimously that workers should be ordered to work harder.

Then the matter of sunlight was raised. In answer to questions, Mo admitted that the sun appeared to be rising later and setting earlier, with a resulting shortening of daylight hours. He had already made some investigation of the matter. "I understand," he said with concern, "that this causes flowers to open later and close earlier. It may indeed account in part for the poor quality and quantity of the present harvest." There were murmurs of agreement from all sides. "In addition," Mo went on, "the afternoons are not as warm as they used to be. There is a quite definite chill in the late afternoon. I feel that it is a grave matter, a very grave matter."

"Then something must be done," shouted an irascible old drone, interrupting while Mo was still speaking.

"Yes, something must," Mo agreed.

But what? He had already checked to ensure that the sun rose at dawn and set at dusk according to the Council's decree. The problem seemed to arise from the fact that dawn and dusk were drawing closer to each other each day. If it continued, there would soon be no sunlight hours at all.

"Should we not direct the sun to rise before dawn and set after dusk?" suggested an intellectual young drone who had hatched only recently, one of the very few drones to emerge from the new brood. There was a hubbub of interested discussion. It was a solution so innovative yet so simple that Mo wondered why he hadn't thought of it himself.

"That's an excellent idea," he said, and raising his voice announced, "as Inspector of Sunlight I will examine the possibility of having the sun rise before dawn and set after dusk."

"When?" asked the irascible old drone.

It was an awkward question. Mo hesitated.

"Well?"

"Tomorrow, I'll look into it tomorrow."

When the meeting was over Mo asked Alfred for his opinion.

"Hmph," Alfred grunted.

"Well, what do you think?"

"About what?"

"Adjusting sunrise and sunset."

"Hmph." Alfred grunted again and said no more. Although he had been moved to speak on the poor quality of the nectar flow, he was preoccupied. For days he had been deeply absorbed in composition. His new Hymn to Life was to be chanted in the Honey Festival Ceremony. It was his longest work yet.

He practiced each morning with the Grand

Drone and a chorus of lesser drones to make sure
that they had memorized it correctly. In the
beginning Daisy kept joining in with his high-
pitched wail, and it was not until the
Grand Drone lost his temper with him that
he finally went away to sulk on a corner of the
threshold.

> Let us praise
> The great Giver of honey
> He has hidden the nectar
> In the willow herb
> He has taught the lowly worker
> To find the blossom,
> To sip and carry and regurgitate
> His nectar,
> Honey of life
> Essence of His Great Dronehood,
> Let us sip His Essence,
> Let us Wallow
> Upon the honeycombs of life,
> And be drunken
> In His name.

The hymn was universally admired, except by Mo. "Can't you see the Grand Drone is just using you, using your gift?" he argued.

"So what?"

"Your little poem about Belle was worth a dozen hymns."

"Poor Belle," Alfred sighed deeply. He knew it would annoy Mo.

Daisy overheard him. "Poor Belle," he wailed from the corner where he had been sulking, "poor dead Belle!"

Some drones began to titter. For most of them, the shock of Mo's disastrous encounter with the wasps had given way to amusement. The episode did have its funny side, not least Mo's shame about it.

"Shut up," Mo muttered in Daisy's direction.

"The drones will be like Belle. Drones too, drones will die," Daisy wailed. It was only Daisy's usual meaningless babble, but each drone who heard felt a sudden chill, as if a cloud had passed between the sun and the earth and cast a shadow over the hive.

"Shut up," half a dozen of them snapped. Daisy stopped in midwail and his voice subsided to a meaningless muttering.

31

mo waited till late morning when the sun stood high in the sky, almost directly above the hive. "I'm going now," he said to Alfred, but Alfred was still preoccupied and did not answer.

Mo flew up to the roof of the hive and considered his first step. It was quite straightforward really. All he had to do was fly up until he reached the sun and then explain the matter in person. He had flown as high as that on nuptial flights, or almost as high.

He looked up and scrutinized the sky. The sun was dazzlingly bright, but that was only to be expected. Naturally, seen from below, it looked impressive, but once he was up there, beside it, he would feel less intimidated. He spread his wings and flew up.

He flew high above the hive and the apple trees, higher than the Norway spruce at the orchard end. He flew up till he could see distant meadows that were lush with after-grass and the green hill beyond. Higher and higher he flew, higher than he had ever flown before. When he grew breathless he paused and hovered till he recovered himself, then flew upward again. He could see the river, a thin ribbon of reflected light, winding between reedy banks and overhanging willows. He saw that beyond the green hill there was another hill and then another. Below him the whole earth stretched out to where it met the sky.

He looked up. The sun was still far away. It seemed no closer than it had been when he was down at the hive. He could still see the hive, a small white speck far below, surrounded by trees that were dotted with yellow apples. He took a deep breath and flew up once more.

The earth grew wider. Spread beneath him now was an entire universe. The fields had shrunk to small patches of yellow and green and the trees were no bigger than bees. He had flown higher than any drone had ever flown before. He could see the universe as no drone had ever seen it.

Yet still above him the sun receded into the infinite blue faster than he could approach it. His wings ached. How much higher could he fly?

While he hovered to recover his breath a passing cloud obscured the sun. The earth and sky turned gray and the air grew cold. The hive was lost to sight in the deep shadows of the orchard. Mo waited impatiently for the sun to reappear, but instead the sky and earth grew darker. He felt a vague unease. The sky was so vast and he was alone, a solitary speck, a single consciousness, in the immense emptiness of the universe. *Why*, he wondered, and was suddenly filled with rage. "Why?" he shouted angrily at the empty sky. "Why?"

It was the essential question, the sum of all of his profound thinking, the end of his quest for understanding. Why is the universe? Why are bees? Why honey? Why life? Why death? "Why?" he raged and then the cloud passed away.

A long sunbeam reached from the sky and bathed him in golden light. He felt its warmth on his wings and its radiance in the hexagonal lenses of his compound eyes. "Why?" he asked again, yearning with all his being to know.

A voice spoke inside his head. It said, *There are only two truths. The first is that the universe is greater than any single bee. The other is that any single bee is greater than the universe.* The sunbeam grew and spread till it illuminated the earth far below. It shone on the orchard and on the white speck that was the hive.

Mo forgot about making sunlight adjustments. Filled with ineffable understanding, he turned and flew back to earth. He was illumined with the light of knowledge. He knew the answers now, all of them. One truth or the other explained everything. The meaning of existence. The existence of meaning. Now, at last, he knew why.

Eagerly he tried to share with others the momentous truths he had discovered. "Alfred, this is important, you must listen," he pleaded.

"Hmph," Alfred said, still preoccupied, and turned away.

"Don't you want to know the ultimate truths?" Mo asked Thora when she was passing by with her honey sac full of nectar.

"Not just now, Mo, another time," she said politely, and hurried inside the hive.

He wandered about trying to find someone who would listen. The workers were working and shooed him away. The drones were busy preparing for the Honey Festival Ceremony which would take place that evening, just before sunset. "Later, Mo," they said, "another time."

the honey Festival Ceremony was not a success. Half a dozen worker bees decided, just when it was about to begin, to carry out repairs to the hive wall at the end of the holy passageway. Sunshine alternating with rain had shrunk the timber and a long crack, caused by winter frosts, had widened almost enough to admit a small enemy. The workers brought propolis and mixed it with resin. They had just begun to fill the hole when the procession entered the passageway.

"Make way, make way," the Grand Drone called out in a loud voice.

"Go away, can't you see we're busy?" a very young worker retorted, "If you want honey ask someone else to get it."

"I don't want honey," the Grand Drone thundered in his immense voice.

"Well, we've no time to groom you either. Go away," a second worker said sharply, pausing an instant in her work.

The Grand Drone was too outraged to speak to them further. He proceeded with the ceremony with as much dignity as he could muster in the face of the disrespectful young workers. Drones crowded into the passageway and tried to ignore the impious chatter of the workers, which persisted right through the ceremony.

"Bang it with your head like this," one said,

demonstrating the best way to pack the resin mixture into the hole.

"Can you give me more wax, the propolis is runny," said another.

"It's an indignity," Alfred whispered to Mo. "How can we chant the hymn with all that noise going on?"

As he spoke a shaft of light lit the darkness. It grew and spread, then suddenly disappeared again. For a few seconds all was dark, and then the light reappeared. For several seconds it came and went intermittently. The workers were not impressed by the miraculous appearance of the light and went on working. They didn't bother to stop, not even when GDS flickered briefly against the wall for an instant before both He and the light disappeared entirely.

"It's him!" Daisy wailed, throwing his usual frenzy of terror at the manifestation of the GDS.

The workers stopped work and watched with interest as Daisy writhed and screamed.

"What's the matter with you?" one of them asked.

"It's him!" Daisy wailed in reply.

"Who?"

"The mouse."

There was a commotion among the drones. Daisy's babblings were meaningless, but some control would have to be exercised over him. He had blasphemed in the Holy Place. A few drones gathered round Daisy, pushing and kicking.

The Grand Drone tried to save what was left of the dignity of the occasion. "The GDS is angered," he announced gravely, "at the unseemly behavior of those who have intruded upon our ceremony. Let us leave this holy place and go and sip honey in His name." The disgruntled drones trundled off to find some ripe honey cells. Only Mo remained in the passageway. For a long time he paced to and fro in deep thought. Daisy, he remembered, had not been born like ordinary drones. He was torn prematurely from his pupa cell on the day that the mouse came into the hive. That was a long time ago. What had made him call out the name of the mouse in the middle of the ceremony?

And then there was the matter of the miraculous light that had accompanied the manifestations of the GDS. Mo had been close enough to the workers to see that their movements to and fro at the crack coincided exactly with the coming and going of the light. It was nothing but sunlight passing through the crack. The crack was in the west wall of the hive where it caught the evening light. That was why the light only appeared in the evening and why there was no light and no manifestation of the GDS on wet evenings. On wet evenings the sunset was overcast with cloud and there could be no golden light.

He examined the crack, which had now been fully repaired. Then he examined the wall, feeling, tasting, and smelling with his sensitive antennae. He felt the bones of the mouse, embalmed in resin and spread-eagled against the wall where the workers had left them because they were too heavy to be carried away.

The meaning was clear. He hurried after the other drones to tell them what he had discovered.

They were drunk. They had gone straight to the honey stores when the ceremony broke up and were roistering now, chanting bits of Alfred's Hymn to Life in slurred voices and staggering along the passageway that led to the brood chamber. Mo's discovery would have to wait till morning.

The young house bees were irritable and cross on the brood comb that night. They pushed and jostled drunken drones who were settling down to sleep.

"This is disgusting," the vociferous young worker complained, "how can we sleep with those nasty drones snoring in the middle of the brood." She pushed and shoved. "Move over," she said to a drone who, stupefied with honey, gave way to her. "I don't see why drones always get the warmest place," she complained, "what use are they to anybody?"

Thora slept on the outer edge of the cluster of bees. Field bees were used to being outdoors and didn't need as much warmth as the hive bees and drones. The nights were growing colder now. Young hive bees felt the chill and clung close to each other for warmth. No wonder they resented the drones. Thora listened to their complaints about the drones taking the warmest place in the brood and wondered why her generation hadn't minded. Of course, drones were needed then, to mate with the Queen. Now their Queen had been mated for life and would mother the hive for a long time to come. She would never need to mate again. The young workers were right, drones weren't needed anymore.

33

in the morning the Grand Drone listened, appalled, to Mo's report of his discovery.

"You say the golden light is only sunlight?"

"That's all. It won't be there anymore. The workers have closed the crack."

"And you claim that the GDS is a dead mouse?" The Grand Drone's voice grew shrill with disbelief.

"Don't you remember, there was a mouse in the hive, a long time ago." Mo looked round. Surely the others could remember? Nobody seemed to.

"Mo, you shouldn't joke about such matters," Alfred said in dismay.

Mo thought of Daisy. Daisy remembered. He had remembered every time he saw the mouse. "Daisy," Mo said, "don't you remember the mouse?"

"Mouse?" Daisy's voice sounded weak and faint.

"Yes, the mouse. It tore you from your cell before you were ready to be born."

"Mouse," Daisy wailed and fell, writhing and kicking on the threshold. Nobody moved to restrain him.

The Grand Drone turned to Mo. "Let you be gone from this place. Let your name be anathema among drones. Let any drone who associates with you be cast out too," he said in a thunderous voice, and a loud hum of approval arose from the other drones.

"It's not fair," Mo protested.

"Begone from this hive," the Grand Drone ordered, and immediately drones gathered round Mo, pushing and jostling, forcing him away from the hive.

"Leave me alone," he shouted angrily, "I'll go myself. Stop pushing." The drones stood back and gave him room to spread his wings. Mo turned to his friend. "Alfred, do you not believe me?" Alfred turned away.

Deeply wounded, Mo flew up from the threshold.

"Wait for me," he heard a plaintive voice call behind him. Daisy had flown up in the air and was following.

"Go back, Daisy," Mo said crossly. "There's no point in your getting yourself into trouble too."

"But I saw it too. I knew all the time, but nobody would listen."

"You don't have to tell them that."

"I want to go with you."

Together they alighted on a leafy hawthorn

branch that was weighted down with green haws. Daisy crawled up and down among the leaves, humming busily and exploring his surroundings. Mo brooded silently.

All day he debated what he should do next. He could go back and apologize for his blasphemy. If he did that the drones might allow him back among them. But to do that he would have to pretend to believe a lie. There was nothing, really, to stop him from going back except his pride. And his personal integrity, of course, or was that just pride with another name?

The hours grew long. "I'm hungry," Daisy announced.

"Then you'd better go back."

"You come too."

"I can't." Mo was very hungry. He longed to go back to the threshold and see what kind of nectar the workers were harvesting today. From where he sat he could see Alfred waylaying one field worker after another and gorging himself. Alfred's betrayal was the worst thing. Now Mo understood a little better how Thora must have felt when she lost her best friend Belle. Which was the worse agony, he wondered, the death of a friend or betrayal by a friend? Betrayal was probably worse, he decided, with profound self-pity.

"You must go back," Daisy said.

"Why?"

"You will miss the destiny of drones."

It would have been funny if they weren't so hungry. Poor Daisy picked up these grand phrases and used them meaninglessly. There was a time when Mo almost believed in the grand destiny of drones, but not anymore. It had all been empty rhetoric. "What destiny? The universe is greater than any individual drone," he murmured, more to himself than to Daisy.

"Tomorrow," Daisy said, nodding wisely, "it will be tomorrow."

"What will be tomorrow?"

"Our destiny. I heard them talking."

"Who?"

"The house bees. The workers. They said to-morrow."

It was more of Daisy's meaningless babble.

"You go and feed," Mo said in a more kindly tone, "I'll stay here."

Daisy flew down to the threshold, and a moment later Thora appeared and alighted on the branch beside Mo.

"What's all this about your being put out of the hive?"

"The Grand Drone has commanded it."

"Pay no attention to him. He can't put anybody out. Do you want honey?" She regurgitated some honey onto her tongue and Mo accepted gratefully. "Who's been tumbling you about?" she asked, noticing his bedraggled appearance, and not waiting for a reply, she brushed and cleaned him till he was shining and handsome again.

Mo noticed how old Thora was growing. Her wings were ragged with use and the feathery hair that had covered the hard chitin shell of her body was worn away, leaving only a smooth shiny surface. He wondered what age she was. At least forty days. For a worker bee, that was old. Drones could live for months on end and a

Queen lived for years, but a worker wore herself out and grew old sooner than any other bee.

"Now come with me," she ordered and flew down to the threshold. Mo followed. Thora glared fiercely at the drones who were still about the threshold, and they made no attempt to interfere with Mo as he passed by them and went inside the hive.

It was wonderful to be back. He had always thought of himself as an independent spirit and did not realize till now how important the security and warmth of the hive was to him. When night fell he gladly found a warm spot on the brood comb among the worker bees and settled down to sleep. He shuddered at the thought of the cold night outside. Another drone snuggled up close to him. "Hi," said Alfred, "you're back, I see."

"Go away and sleep with your new friends," Mo said indignantly, turning his tail end to him.

"It wasn't much fun without you," Alfred said agreeably.

"Some friend you turned out to be."

"Sorry."

"That's all right." Mo tried to sound grudging but he was glad to have a friend again. Together they pushed and squeezed into a warm spot where workers were clustered closely.

The hive bees were irate to find two drones among them. "Get into the middle with the other drones," they said, and several pushed and poked at them, trying to make them move to the center of the cluster where the drones belonged.

"Leave them alone," Thora said, "they're with me."

"But we have things to talk about," the house bees protested.

"What things?"

"We can't discuss it in front of drones. You know what we mean."

"It's all right. You can talk in front of Mo and Alfred."

"Won't they mind?"

"Perhaps, but what can they do?"

Thora clung close to Mo and Alfred to reassure them a little. Alfred didn't really need reassurance.

He was asleep and snoring already. He had been slightly drunk on honey that evening and would have been asleep long ago, except that he had been looking for Mo. Mo, however, was wide awake and listening. Thora thought on the whole that it was better he should know. He had always been the most reasonable of the drones. He would understand why the workers must do what they were going to do.

The matter was debated intensely. "It must be tomorrow," a young worker said firmly. "There is no point in waiting. We put it off from day to day and all the time we are wasting winter supplies."

"We cannot allow any more plundering of the honey stores," another young bee agreed.

"Can't it wait a few days," an older bee argued, "let them live another little while?"

"What harm have they done?" someone asked.

"What use are they?" several younger bees retorted at once.

"What do they mean?" Mo whispered to Thora. "Who are they talking about?"

"Drones," answered Thora.

"What are they going to do?"

"Send all of you away."

"Where?"

"Outside."

"When?"

"Tomorrow."

She stroked his head and wings to show him that it wasn't personal, that it was simply something that had to be done. She felt him tremble a little as he realized the full implications of what was being discussed around him.

Thora had known for days that it must happen. Everyone in the hive knew except for the drones themselves, who had been too busy with their ceremonies and Council meetings to notice. Some young bees had already been refusing point-blank to feed or groom them. However the older bees had obliged for old time's sake. Now that must end. Already, in the mornings, there was a chill in the air, and a heavy dew gave evidence of the first frost. The nights were growing perceptibly longer and the hours of sunlight shorter. The main honey flow had ended and field bees brought home less and less nectar with each passing day. Today Thora had found some Michaelmas daisies blooming in a garden, but tomorrow where would she find honey? The hive could not afford to feed hundreds of hungry drones forever. The young workers were right, what use were they? Even Mo. He had served his purpose.

34

although the decision was already made, the workers deferred to the Queen and let her have the last word on the matter. "A few of them are my sons," she said sadly.

"Yes, but you will have more sons," her attendants reassured her.

"Then let it be done if it must," she said, sighing deeply. She sat silent on the brood comb for a long time. Now that summer had drawn to an end she laid fewer eggs, and would soon lay none at all until the first spring flowers came again. There were enough young bees in the hive for the winter cluster, and enough honey and pollen stores to provide for them. That was all that mattered for now.

"Yes," said the Queen, sighing again, "you may proceed. It is time."

"Yes," each worker agreed, and some, like Thora, grieved for the loss of the gentle, ridiculous males who had been their companions during the long days of summer.

In the morning the drones slept late. When they wakened and approached young house bees, extending their tongues to be fed, they were refused. When they danced grooming invitations they were ignored. Growing hungry, they headed for the honeycombs behind the brood chamber, but the young bees lined up in phalanx formation to bar their entry.

The drones reacted with bewilderment.

"But we always have honey when we waken," Alfred explained again and again to any worker who looked less fierce than the others.

"Not anymore," they replied. "You must leave the hive. Drones eat too much. The hive cannot afford to go on feeding you."

"The drones must go," Daisy wailed, "their destiny has come."

Destiny. Mo heard the word and for the first time he understood what it meant. Daisy had known all along. He was the only drone who had understood from the beginning. Daisy, the drone who was not quite drone, knew what the rest were too blind, too pompous, or too vain to see. And now their moment of destiny had come.

He could see it all now. Every bee had its destiny. The Queen was the mother of the hive, yet her destiny was not really glorious. She would serve the hive, laying eggs endlessly till one day, when the hive was rich and prosperous, she would sacrifice all to the future and go with a swarm to start again, to create another colony in another place. The workers' destiny was even more arduous. They toiled endlessly and their lives were short. They worked themselves to death laying in stores that they would never eat and rearing young for a future that they themselves would not live to see. Theirs was a destiny made up of innumerable small sacrifices every day of their brief lives. And now the drones, who had been so drunken, so vainglorious, so earthy and crude, the moment of their destiny had come and what a noble destiny it would be. They had been the favored ones of the hive, allowed to enjoy all the pleasures of existence. Now they were asked to go, to starve or die of cold for the sake of the hive. Their lives were to culminate in one supremely noble moment of self-sacrifice. Mo felt a peculiar sense of joy at the prospect.

"Listen to me," he said, raising his voice and speaking for other drones to hear. They ceased their demands for honey and listened in silent dismay. "Fellow drones, you must immediately stop this unseemly squabbling. The hour of our destiny has come. Our destiny is glorious. We are asked to sacrifice our lives for the good of the hive."

There were murmurs of indignation. Mo ignored them and went on speaking. "Every one of us has enjoyed a full and happy life, but now we live at the expense of the hive. The honey that we consume is needed for the future of the hive. Let us go bravely. Let us make the sacrifice of our lives willingly. We can go nobly or we can be driven ignominiously. The choice is ours. Let our destiny be a glorious one."

There was a shocked silence. Drones looked from one to another trying to understand what Mo was saying. "Why should we sacrifice our lives," several drones asked. "Why can't the workers sacrifice theirs?"

"Because it's our destiny, our noble destiny," Mo explained.

"Nonsense," the Grand Drone said in a voice that was shrill with fear, "I demand honey." He turned to a worker. "I demand honey," he said again and then retreated nervously before her fierce glare.

"Let us go," Mo said. He turned and walked resolutely to the entrance. A few drones, inspired by his noble purpose, followed.

"Wait for me," Daisy called, and hurried after them.

"Can't I have just a little bit of honey before I go?" Alfred pleaded to a worker.

"No."

He saw Thora passing through the throng, bringing home her first harvest of the morning. "Thora, won't you give me some nectar?" Surely Thora wouldn't refuse him. He stood in front of her, his tongue extended.

"I'm sorry, Alfred, there's no more to spare." It grieved her to refuse Alfred, but feeding him would only prolong his agony. It was kinder to refuse.

"It's so hard to be noble when you're hungry," he pleaded. "If I could have just a little honey I would be brave."

"No, you can't have any."

Unwillingly Alfred turned and went to the entrance. Thora, with a sinking heart, watched him go. He paused to cast a last despairing look at the paradise that he was about to lose. The smell of honey hung heavily in the air. The dim amber darkness of the hive had never seemed more beautiful. "Please!" he begged one last time.

"No!" the workers chorused.

Most drones could not bring themselves to make the noble sacrifice. The Grand Drone had to be dragged out forcibly to the threshold, and some who resisted more violently were stung to death and their unwieldy corpses thrown out on the dewy grass.

The day was long. Hungry drones hummed dolefully and hovered about the threshold in bewilderment. The field workers who still came and went had to threaten with their stings when drones persisted in their demands for honey. From time to time a few drones tried to rush the entrance but the guard bees were fierce and uncompromising. No drone could enter.

Evening came and then night. The drones were left outside. They tried to make a cluster on the wall of the hive but the night air closed around them and chilled them through.

"I'm cold," Daisy wailed, and he went on wailing till his voice grew faint and was heard no more.

Mo stayed close to Alfred, encouraging him to be noble, to die with dignity.

"Life was so sweet," Alfred said wistfully.

"Yes, but now it's over. We have to accept that."

"If I could taste honey just one more time."

"We have had our share of honey."

"That's true," Alfred agreed sadly. He was silent for a long time.

Mo, feeling life ebbing from his wings and legs, wondered if Alfred were already dead. Then, unexpectedly, he felt him stirring at his side.

"Mo, are you awake?" Alfred asked.

"Yes."

"I have composed another poem. Do you want to hear it?"

"Of course."
Alfred recited it softly.

> Life is
> A sip of honey
> Yesterday.

"Well, what do you think?"
Mo sighed deeply. "It is sublime, truly sublime."
"Yes, I think it is," Alfred agreed happily, and did not speak again.

deep in the warmth of the hive, Thora was unable to sleep. Her thoughts were with Mo and Alfred outside in the cold night. Were they still alive or had they succumbed to hunger and cold? She was deeply despondent. Now her last friends were gone and she was old. Soon she would be dead too. She had made the worker's sacrifice, the small daily sacrifices of time and strength, day after day. Now she was an old bee with no future. She bowed her head and wished it was all over.

In the morning the threshold was littered with the corpses of drones. House bees briskly cleared them away and returned inside. Thora, setting out on her first foraging trip of the day, looked for Alfred and Mo among the dead and found them side by side, friends in death as in life.

Sad-hearted, she flew away. She flew a long way. She was tired, very tired. She had slept badly, fretting about Alfred and Mo. Now her wings ached and moved clumsily in the cold morning air. She flew down by the river. On the riverbank could sometimes be found flowers that bloomed late in the milder air of the river. She found a few purple loosestrife growing among the reeds and sipped nectar there.

Farther along the riverbank she came across a wild briar twined about a hawthorn tree. From it hung a solitary white rose, its petals a little frayed and browned at the edges, its scent faded. It reminded Thora of something, something that happened a long time ago. She tried hard to remember. The rose had a single dewdrop on one of its petals. Hadn't she once drunk from a dewdrop like that one? She sipped a little now and then she rested, right in the heart of the rose. It would do no harm to rest a little while. She was so very tired and so old.

The sun rose in the sky and the air grew warm. A light breeze stirred the air and the rose rocked to and fro. It was pleasant to be cradled in a rose, to have no cares and no responsibilities. Then she remembered. Idleness. She was being idle. Alfred had explained it a long time ago. It wasn't so difficult after all. It was just that she had never really had time to be idle, even though she had so much wanted to be.

The hive was far away, too far away. She might never go back. What did it matter now, one old bee more or less? She would never be missed. There was nobody waiting for her there, not anymore.

The breeze stirred. A single petal detached

itself from the rose and fell to the ground. Thora thought of Belle, always busy, thinking only of the hive. Whatever would Belle say, if she could see her now? "The petal, in the breath of a summer breeze, falls to the ground," she murmured because the words had come into her head.

The noonday sun shone warmly on her old, hairless body and on her ragged wings. What did it matter now, what did anything matter except the sunlight and the flowers and the gentle breeze that rocked her to and fro.

About this Scholastic Signature author

SOINBHE LALLY is the recipient of the prestigious Hennessy Literary Award and was shortlisted for the Reading Association of Ireland Award. Her short fiction, plays, and essays have appeared on both sides of the Atlantic in such journals as the *Atlantic Monthly* and the *Irish Press*.

A Hive for the Honeybee, her first novel to be published in the United States, has been nominated for the Bisto Book of the Year — one of Ireland's top literary prizes.

Soinbhe Lally lives in Donegal, Ireland.